T0017901

PRAISE .

Meeting in Positano

"Set amid the landscape of the enchanting, evolving Amalfi Coast, *Meeting in Positano* pays homage to the mystifying and impenetrable affection between two women. It is like reading a love letter from the past, one rife with the truths about friendship that most of us wouldn't dare utter aloud: desire, envy, nostalgia, adoration. Complex and evocative, this story is not to be missed."

—Sarah Penner, author of *The Lost Apothecary*

"*Meeting in Positano* is an absolute dream of a novel. Set on the magical Amalfi Coast, it is full of beauty and yearning, secrets and art. The friendship at the novel's center is so compelling, and ultimately heartbreaking, I felt I was swept along with Goliarda and Erica, by the dazzling sea, through the Positano nights."

—Luanne Rice, *New York Times* bestselling author of *The Shadow Box*

"Goliarda Sapienza's *Meeting in Positano* is a gorgeously written meditation on female friendship and human connection, as well as a lyrical ode to Positano, one of the most enchanting places in the world. This lovely book, full of joy, nostalgia, and tragedy, is not to be missed."

—Alyssa Palombo, author of *The Borgia Confessions*

ALSO BY GOLIARDA SAPIENZA

The Art of Joy

OTHER PRESS / NEW YORK

· MEETING IN ·
Positano

GOLIARDA SAPIENZA

TRANSLATED FROM THE ITALIAN BY BRIAN ROBERT MOORE

Originally published in Italian as *Appuntamento a Positano* in 2015
by Giulio Einaudi editore, Torino, Italy.
Copyright © 2015 The Estate of Goliarda Sapienza
Published in agreement with
Piergiorgio Nicolazzini Literary Agency (PNLA).

Translation copyright © 2021 Other Press

This book was translated thanks to a grant awarded by the
Italian Ministry of Foreign Affairs and International Cooperation.

Special thanks to Le Tripode for preparing the original French version of the "Life of
Goliarda Sapienza" section on pages 237–249. Translated by Adriana Hunter. Photos
courtesy of the Estate of Goliarda Sapienza.

Production editor: Yvonne E. Cárdenas
Text designer: Jennifer Daddio / Bookmark Design & Media Inc.
This book was set in Filosofia by
Alpha Design & Composition of Pittsfield NH

3 5 7 9 10 8 6 4 2

Library of Congress Cataloging-in-Publication Data
Names: Sapienza, Goliarda, author. | Moore, Brian Robert, 1992- translator.
Title: Meeting in Positano / Goliarda Sapienza ; translated from the Italian
by Brian Robert Moore.
Other titles: Appuntamento a Positano. English
Description: New York : Other Press, 2021. | Originally published in Italian
as Appuntamento a Positano in 2015 by Giulio Einaudi editore, Torino.
Identifiers: LCCN 2020041158 (print) | LCCN 2020041159 (ebook) |
ISBN 9781635420432 (trade paperback) | ISBN 9781635420449 (ebook)
Classification: LCC PQ4879.A675 A73513 2021 (print) |
LCC PQ4879.A675 (ebook) | DDC 853/.914—dc23
LC record available at https://lccn.loc.gov/2020041158
LC ebook record available at https://lccn.loc.gov/2020041159

Everyone was held spellbound as she walked down the steps to the dock where a skiff waited for her to push out to sea. Or when upon her return, at no later than one o'clock, Nicola—the son of Lucibello, called the Monkey, the oldest and most audacious ex-fisherman in Positano, who like the rest of them had switched to renting beach umbrellas and loungers—helped her down from the boat, and with admiring eyes followed her steps on the carpet of wooden planks which made a snug living room of the ancient, rocky bay.

Every time, Nicola was left breathless by that "thank you," barely whispered from two harmoniously shaped lips, perhaps too full to be perfect. The teenage boy couldn't help but stare until she went out of view, slightly hurrying up the large steps through the feverish and bustling crowd, the men all in trunks, the women in their beach outfits, too colorful to bear the contrast with her sober sarong or her trouser pants.

He had never seen her go swimming, even though he had attended to her since he was a child, the boy ruminated as he jumped onto the princess's boat to tie it up. To go swimming with her, what he would give for that. He threw one last jealous glance at the friends, who always surrounded her like a faithful band, protecting her, or cutting her off from the rest of the world. If only he could be one of them, he thought as he tidied up the boat, collecting with care the precious objects that those lucky people always forgot: sun cream, a watch, a bracelet.

The princess sent him daydreaming. He couldn't even say how many countesses, duchesses, and princesses he'd seen. But that one! Lying in the tidied boat, Nicola dreams of her, his brown body curled up in the sun, his lionlike head on a muscular arm with skin, in the hollow of the armpit, that's still as soft as a baby's.

Lightly and confidently walking around the veranda of the Buca di Bacco, crowded at that hour with people having a drink, Erica absentmindedly ignores all of those faces that inevitably turn to watch her. And if at a certain point her gaze stops for a minute, it is to greet with a nod Antonio and Michele, two old waiters at the café who have known her since she was a little girl.

"So you lied to me, Antonio. You do know her. She waved

to you. A bit thin for my tastes. Who is she?" asks a very tan young man with a dazzling smile.

"She's not for you, boss. But if I may, take a look around . . . Don't you see how many blossoming girls there are? Now that they're in season, of course . . ."

"In season?" the young man presses him, intrigued, partly because he has heard about the head waiter at the Buca di Bacco and his zesty jokes, as they say in Naples, and he's anxious to hear at least one of them to tell his friends during the long Milanese winter.

"Oh, you know, they only last a summer. They come here in June, they bloom by mid-August, and then, withered, they disappear with the first rains. A magnificent crop this year. Take advantage of it. The grapes don't always grow the same way twice."

"Fine, but what about her?"

"She's something special. That kind of woman is born only once every hundred years, and maybe there won't be any more of them. Nature has lost the mold. But like I said, she's not for you."

"I might be a little bit offended."

"What do you mean? I don't say it to offend you, but it's something else you want! Just last year Signorina Erica rejected an English duke."

"Ah, she's not married? She didn't seem all that young to me."

"She's been a widow for three years, and she has no interest in remarrying."

"How old is she? Does she have any kids?"

"No kids. And as far as her age goes—who knows?"

"Sure you know. I saw how sweetly she acknowledged you!"

"Listen, I'm not for the death penalty, but I'd accept it just for one crime."

"Which?"

"Saying a beautiful woman's age."

"Now that's a good one!"

The young man laughs, now turning to the friends who have been following the conversation. I'm also listening, amused, and knowing Prandino's typically Lombard stubbornness, I wait to hear what his waiter friend's reply will be. But for once I see his eyes give in, surrendering to Antonio, and his blue-green irises grow melancholy. Following his gaze, I notice that his melancholy is due to the curvy figure that has walked with a dancelike pace up the wide steps guarded on both sides by two haughty marble lions keeping watch over the town (perhaps put there to terrify the Saracen raiders of the past?) and who now stands nearly bent over to speak to a short and stocky local girl—a waitress or a salesgirl from one of the many pants stores that recently sprouted up in the town. The girl doesn't seem at all intimidated by her, and after a few moments the woman even plants two kisses on her face before running off. Now, even lighter than before, she flies across the narrow opening which unfolds like a Renaissance theater with its small surrounding shops, and she disappears, to the right, into a forever shadowy alley.

Prandino sits in silence near me. Maybe he too is following with his imagination the route that apparition is tracing. She might have stopped to look in a shop window, and since Antonio says she's a habitué of Positano, she is probably still chatting with that woman Kabalevska, the Russian fabric designer who arrived here twenty years ago for a three-day vacation and never left the town since.

Precisely because of the fame of Positano, we had come along with our director Maselli and his screenwriter, Prandino Visconti, to see if it could work as the setting for the film we were writing, *Abandoned*. But only a few hours in the town had convinced us that it was too beautiful and enchanted for a story like ours. We were just talking about this, having a drink at the Buca di Bacco, when we were momentarily distracted by the woman's appearance. I remember what Maselli said, so wry and witty back then.

"You can never be off your guard these days . . . As soon as you're sure that modern mass society has leveled everything, there before you appears a vision of the past. I mean, who is she? Anna Karenina? Like something from another world. You like her, huh, Prando? I prefer these modern girls in blue jeans. Fewer problems—or maybe not, but at least they're new problems."

His director's eye was not wrong about Princess Erica, because I was also struck by her aura as she strode through the blue and gold of that slice of sea, vast like an ocean yet calm and silent like a lake. That night, my bags already packed to go back to Rome, I took advantage of the time the director gave us for dinner and asked for some information from Giacomino, the owner of the oldest restaurant in Positano, who for no apparent reason had taken to me, and whom, as sometimes happens, I felt like I had known forever.

"Oh, the young princess! It's no great mystery. You women today take work too seriously, reducing yourselves to tomboys. No offense, but what do you get out of those tense faces and trouser pants? Not that it's any of my business if the world is turning upside down... She could be more or less your age, thirty, thirty-two years old. I saw her grow up, summer after summer. When she was just a little thing she'd come with her family in a carriage. That's right, back then the road leading down to the town was a kind of dirt trail, and the prince preferred to leave the car up at Santa Maria and rent a carriage. He was an educated man of great tradition."

As the woman moved out of view, calm was restored in our group. Maybe she doesn't exist, she's a ghost, I told myself while I listened to Maselli: "This town is too picturesque, coming here was useless. We have to go straight back to Rome and start looking again for the right place for us and for our protagonists in *Abandoned*. I'd thought that the story could take place in the south, but you're right, Prando, it's in the north and only in the north, even if the characters' isolation from the historical context of '44 would be more warranted in the south. Now let's go pack and get out of here."

2

I forgot the charm of Positano and of all of its inhabitants from that time, and maybe I never would have remembered any of it if, a few years later, we hadn't gone back down to shoot a documentary on the Landing of the Saracens, the great celebration that every year on the fifteenth of August consumes all of the residents of the Amalfi Coast.

I was running through narrow streets looking for extras, up and down steep steps that jostle your laziness and your imagination into a single, dreamlike dizziness. That's when, turning at one of the countless corners glaring with sunlight, I almost run right into her. Startled, I stop myself just in time from striking her like a fury—the fury of a movie big shot. (I'm lower than her, and

I need to look up in order to check that she hasn't actually been hurt by my head.) Her broad face is illuminated by two eyes that are so big and elongated, as if stretched toward her temples, that I go quiet, even if I know I should be apologizing. Sure enough, she is waiting, staring at me attentively. In her honey-colored gaze shine golden flakes of mirth, while her full head of ash-blond curls whipping lightly against her cheeks and neck seems moved to reproach, albeit tenderly. It's almost as though she now finds herself having to scold a naughty kid rather than an adult. That fluttering, which says, *Careful, child,* makes me feel like what I probably am: a clumsy little girl, and maybe a dirty one, too. Meanwhile she smells of jasmine or some similar perfume.

I overcome the embarrassment that has constricted my body and my voice, and manage to say, "Pardon me." She replies with a voice that echoes as clear as crystal: "That's all right, it happens when you're new to Positano. You can't run in this town." A strange feeling of peace, as when as a child you're forgiven by your mother, floods through my limbs. I'm about to say something back just to hear that voice again, when I realize that her face is already outside my line of vision. She has turned her back to me. I see her in her long white skirt glide down the stairs, ethereal and seemingly lit by her own inner light. I have just enough time to glimpse her bare feet, elongated but strong, arched like a dancer's, when in a flash I recognize the woman I had seen cross the beach years before, hypnotizing everyone with her stride.

Part of the beauty of working in film is that if you want to, you can establish relationships with everyone wherever you go, or at least that was the way things were in the fifties, when our movie industry was still at an avant-garde stage and relatively free from the influence of business. Most of all, films were made out in the streets and in towns. Taking advantage of this perk, I started to seek out information on that woman. Even for someone like me, who was used to being around the likes of Nazim Hikmet, Luchino Visconti, Joyce Lussu—or the beautiful and brilliantly talented Anna Magnani, Lucia Bosé, and Rina Morelli—it was tough to get her out of my head.

She was hardly ever seen around the town. In the month we spent in Positano, I could get a glimpse of her only three times, and always from afar.

Giacomino Senior—legendary cook of Positano, who at ninety-five years old still basked on the sunny steps next to one of the large stone lions, at times looking like an in-the-flesh copy of those statues, especially when he'd doze off—once said to me: "I haven't spent much time with the princess because I stopped working twenty years ago. I handed everything down to my son, Giacomino...He's the one you need to talk to. I can tell you about her father, a great man! Not because he was a nobleman—this town is swimming in those—but because he was like a learned professor, who everyone respected. He was my first client when this beach was still nothing but rocks. I'd learned to cook on board the boats. When I was twelve my parents had to send me off so we wouldn't starve, but I got tired of the sea and adventures—I'd sailed for twenty years! So, in the hollow of the rocks, right there where the Buca di Bacco is today, with four tables, an oven I made with my own hands, and fish I'd catch myself, I opened Positano's first osteria. The prince was a liberal type, and he'd come with his wife, an educated woman who spoke to men just like a man, and with their three daughters. All three of them were beautiful. When they'd arrive by carriage people would even run just to see how lovely they were ... But go up and ask my son Giacomo now that they've turned off the lights ... Princess Erica must be the second to last of the Beneventanos."

"Oh, Signorina, the charm of little Beneventano!" Like a slightly more sophisticated echo of his father, his big lion's head a bit more delicate but with the same sharp-witted blue eyes, Giacomino Junior tells me: "In my opinion it's all thanks to old-fashioned rearing."

"But her father was a liberal," I interrupt him, sure and foolish like nearly all of my young generation, which had fallen for the illusion of unstoppable progress.

"Yeah, of course, the liberal son of liberal parents. He was never Fascist, if that's what you mean. But in the home, with his daughters, he was old-fashioned ... You could say that I nourished them. Their villa was too high for them to keep going up and down every day. The daughters and the young English lady had a table reserved for them. I can still see them all there, happy and beautiful! So much chatting and laughter around that table! But they were always polite. The prince would even make me a weekly list of their

meals, all simple food. They could only have dessert on
Sunday, for instance. To me, that's what is so captivating
in Erica. She was brought up the old-fashioned way, they
never tainted her with overly dry studies . . . Take yourself"
(over time I had managed to get that philosopher-cook—
who was also gifted in the art of remembering, perhaps
the most difficult art of all—to speak to me quite casually),
"you would be a beautiful woman if only . . ."

"If only what, Giacomino? You know you can say anything to me."

"There, that's the problem! With you it's like talking
to another guy . . . It's not right, going against nature like
that. What are all these women after, dying to work just
as we poor men have to? Don't they understand that it's
all been the will of the barons of industry? As you know,
my work takes me to New York every other year. I've seen
with my own eyes how women have been seduced by what
they call democracy: they toil like slaves, and they believe
that tomorrow after all that toil they'll have earned other
people's respect. You're all wrong—fodder for factories and
for war, that's what they've made women into. I might not
know much, but I see the hidden designs and I've got a good
memory. That's partly what saved me from Fascism and
from the war . . ."

I let him talk, I know that at this point I won't be getting
any more precise information about her. There's nothing
you can do once Giacomino starts philosophizing. Now he's
talking of the money god that the Americans have foisted
on the world, of Ezra Pound whom he met, and of how his

own Positano will be destroyed by the wide road that local merchants have decided to open at their own expense, cutting through the mountains.

"Look, the wound still hasn't healed from that damned asphalt road they opened in the twenties, and they already want to widen it."

He's had me stand up and look at the mountain. Perhaps due to the evocative sadness that has taken hold of his voice, I feel like I can even see it bleeding up there where an asphalt line cuts through carob, olive, and orange trees, with no regard for the wild chaos of massive rocks. The mountain is still beautiful, but how much longer can it last? When they've widened the road, who will save us from the landslide of cars and people hungry for pleasures once reserved for the few?

"Signorina, I'll be honest, you look like a young boy who's grown up too fast from all of life's troubles, whereas my Erica must be more or less your age, and just look at how she flies down the steps with her sister Olivia. Olivia was the most beautiful of the three jewels of the Beneventano family. The eldest, Fiore, killed herself. Oh yeah, all of the most beautiful things have a secret sorrow. There's no escaping nature: too much beauty conceals sorrow. Take the cactus flower, it only lasts a night. Or gardenias, or jasmine . . . The Beneventano women, with their beauty, carry an inner sadness."

That evening I tried to instill my own interest in that secret sadness conveyed by Giacomino in our director and in the other members of the crew staying in that neat little hotel perched on top of one of the many peaks that like a luminous ray delineate Positano at night. That woman was in such a precarious balance between the ancient and the modern, and seemed so emblematic to me in her decision to live nearly year-round in a place that was still isolated from the barbaric advances of products, merchandise, and urban madness. Too romantic, too much of an "extreme case," was the laconic response I received from those sweet, Togliattian* guerrilla fighters.

Maybe they're right, I thought as I walked out onto the balcony of the eagle's nest cradling us. I was not going to waste any more time on my own weakness for bourgeois individualism, which, I could now see, that woman had reawakened in me. But then, in front of the lights plummeting down from the cliffs in kaleidoscopic patterns, the memory of her smile spurred me to go out and look for her, through the piazza, the street corners, the narrow alleys, all the way down to the shore with its lights glowing against the dark of the sea.

But I did not find her.

---

* Palmiro Togliatti (1893–1964) was an Italian Communist politician who, in exile in the Soviet Union, supported Italian Resistance fighters during the Second World War and later served in postwar governments. The narrator's film crew and social set are active leftists who sided with the Resistance to the Fascists during the war.

3

In Rome that winter I tried to track down what
by then seemed to me to be merely a ghost, a figure that, partly to make fun of myself, I started
to refer to in my thoughts as my very own "extreme case." I didn't confess it to anyone in that
era of political activism, when even a count like
Luchino Visconti didn't concern himself with
anyone but fishermen and factory workers. On
more than one occasion he had urged me in that
sharp way of his not to isolate myself too much in
the "personal" while there was the great medium
of film to help educate the multitudes. Why didn't
I act anymore? Why didn't I use my talent to influence the ideological direction we could give to
the masses? No, Mario Alicata was the one who
said that, but back then Visconti and Alicata were

always together. To me, the daughter of a criminal lawyer, brought up in an antechamber crowded with characters who were all "extreme cases" and stacks of papers that told only of other exceptionalities, that curious creature whom everyone in Positano loved—something already rare in and of itself—always fluttered at the edges of my imagination, like a meeting that I could not miss.

I met the painter Lorenzo Tornabuoni through his sister, Lietta, a journalist I had known since the end of the war. He owned a house in Positano, and loved that place with all of the tender and furious excess of his artistic talent. He introduced me to Landy Morgan, who was also a painter, an American who had been in Positano for more than twenty years and was close to this woman of mine.

In his small studio, in the shadow of the damp green of old trees, Landy seems like more of a friar than a painter—but one of those ancient, hardy friars, who used to spend more time in the fields than at the easel. In his Bostonian English mixed with a Neapolitan accent, he declares: "You could say that Erica has helped half the town, myself included in some way. Helping didn't mean just lending money or teaching some little barefoot girl. She was the first one to believe in these nonsensical paintings of mine in an age marked by the shattering of the image, of sound, of the soul. She was the first to buy one of my paintings, and every time I go to see her I am astounded to still see it hanging in her bedroom. She must have really liked it after all. To this day she helps me feel confident—even if my paintings are now highly valued in New York, an artist's self-doubt, as you know, stays like an unhealed wound from his early failures, always lying in wait, ready to open again."

Listening to Landy as he raised a troubadour's love song to his lady, I became more and more convinced that he would not introduce me to her, the same way he never introduced Lorenzo. But what did it matter? It was so pleasant to be in his house, and I felt so happy during those years in my solitary search for words, verses, poems, that I was almost content with that inconclusive meeting. And then there was another reason for my feeling satisfied at the time: while going in search of a single face, I discovered an entire little world which, as I would later realize, was at the core of so many changes that had begun to stir underground in our country. But all of that happened later. Then, in that sweet early afternoon fragrant with coffee, in front of the nonconformist masterpieces that Landy showed me, I decided I would no longer look for my princess. Instead I would focus on enjoying—sometimes for a week, sometimes for a few months—that town which I had found was not only an aerie-like plaything at night and a sacred Mediterranean altar in the morning, but a true crossroads of international customs, languages, and races.

As is always the case when traveling, you only uncover the soul of a town in people's homes. And so I went from house to house, moving from the humblest—the home of the ex-fisherman Lucibello, where in the winter I'd go to eat lentil-and-endive soup—to the terrace of Irma and Edna, two beautiful American women who could have been anywhere from sixty to one hundred, it was impossible to say. There, at night, dinner was served among painters, sculptors, or simple wanderers from all over the world, both rich and poor. One evening I met a Japanese nobleman who looked so ragged he could have passed for a tramp.

It was at Irma and Edna's that I met my first existentialists. They didn't reflect the old style of the gloomy Parisian haunts, but were of a completely different nature, purely in search of joy in their colored tatters. They were already presaging the era of hope of the hippies and flower children. One of them was named Wally. The eyes on her beautiful, still-childlike face were always accented with black, as in mourning, although she told me it was only to mock the put-on suffering of types like Merleau-Ponty, Sartre, and Juliette Gréco. She made a living in Positano dancing in the upscale clubs.

She was such a stupendous, possessed girl, Wally: twirling from one end of the large dance floor to the other, while some hints of hashish and marijuana already quivered amid gasps of enthusiasm and emotion, an aroma so similar to freshly cut hay, which like a steady breeze gladdened the walls, the pergolas, the steps awash with sunlight in the morning or with the pristine milk of the moon under the night's endless sky.

Some of the young painters clearly didn't shy away from the stuff. Like Hans, with his gaunt, Byzantine Christ's face and long straw-colored hair bouncing to the rhythm of the town's steps. The local kids jokingly called him "the

Crucifix." "Look how bony he is, he's only missing the iron nails!" He sold his faux-naïf paintings by hanging them on the long walls that sloped down to the town's only piazza. But who could have suspected then that the pleasing scent of hay permeating his jeans even in the early morning was the faint sign of the coming of another dreadful era (another war?) that was starting to be unleashed from above onto our towns? No one could have, least of all me, as I walked serenely down that narrow street all the way to the marina, the melodic conclusion of an architectural symphony.

I had a precious date with my little boat for one. Though it was much sought after, Teresa Lucibello always reserved that light, maneuverable vessel for me whenever I was in Positano. With it I explored the small beaches that opened out like the wings of an endless stage, sometimes rough and ravinelike, sometimes as cozy and welcoming as shells dug out by the expert work of the waves.

Led by a desire for peace after wasting away in the city, I have finally come ashore, and I'm still looking for the sister of the giant shell encircling me—one that is smaller and more tranquil, still speckled with coral—when I am suddenly stopped by an apparition (am I still sleeping?): a naked beauty the likes of which I've never seen before, and on a beach so exposed to the candid light of the clear April sun, her head gently turned to avoid the slanted rays shimmering off of the sea.

I observe her profile, with her perfect forehead, a nose and jaw that, even if they do harmoniously complement her forehead, are just a little too pronounced. A strange feeling of embarrassment takes hold of me at the thought that she is sleeping and that I am staring at her nude body like a thief, with no right to do so. Slowly, and just like a thief, I turn around and start to flee toward my boat.

Back then on the Coast, there was an unwritten law: never come ashore on a beach that's already occupied. There was plenty of space for the few regulars who frequented the area. Many of them, when they didn't arrive in a boat, would even leave a clearly visible sign of their presence by the shore's edge: a pair of sandals, a towel, a book.

There was no object when I came ashore, I tell myself to allay the insane sensation that I'm a thief. I look around one more time to be sure, but there's nothing. Probably her skiff was in need of repair and one of the Lucibellos brought her in another boat. I'm about to set out again in my boat when I hear a voice, one that I recognize by now.

"Signorina, I'm sorry, you wouldn't by chance have any sun cream you could lend me? I forgot mine on the boat, and the sun is very strong. We haven't had such a beautiful April in years."

I listen to that voice, but I only look down at my feet. While not ugly, they are too big for my height, and too tan compared to those mystical toes barely glazed by the sun that are now resting right in front of me on the small stretch of sand. My feet, I continue to think stubbornly, look like Nicola Lucibello's. Like him, I'm "in love" with this woman, and I don't want my eyes to catch her naked form again by looking up: I wouldn't want to come across as one of those not unlikable but ostentatiously masculine lesbians who no longer have to hide behind fake feminine manners.

"Yes, I do," I hear myself answer, and, after a second, I realize I am moving toward her, thankfully in an easy, natural way. I note that in spite of everything, I've managed to maintain a completely neutral demeanor. I make my mind up to look at her. How could I have doubted her refinement? She's not brazenly nude in front of me, but fully wrapped in a large, light-blue sarong, which shapes itself to her body like an evening dress. The color is reflected in her eyes: they aren't honey-colored as they'd first appeared to me, but blue like the cloth covering her.

"I'll only take a drop and I'll give it right back."

"No, no!" I reply, perhaps too quickly. "By all means, keep it. I'm not planning to swim. I just arrived yesterday and I'm too tired to ... Oh, you know, the exhausting work of the movie business. It's becoming a real nightmare. All the things you need to worry about ..." What in the world am I telling this stranger? Why this avalanche of confessions? If I don't stop, I'll come off as a windbag, maybe an even less desirable impression than that of the novice lesbian. "...and soon I'm going to go play a part in Luchino Visconti's new film, up in Venice ..."

Now even the name-dropper comes out in me unexpectedly, and who knows what else would next, if not for her stopping me.

"Clearly you're tired! I'll hold on to it then, thank you. It's exactly the one I use. But I don't mean to keep you. To give it back, I can—"

"Oh, it doesn't matter!" I respond, while thinking at the same time: What kind of moron am I? I tried so hard to meet this woman, and now that I get the chance to be with her, I throw it away like a stupid idiot—that's what Nicola would say if he were here.

"Stupid, stupid, stupid."

"What did you say?" she asks, whether smiling or saddened, I can't tell. "Listen, how about this: I'm always in my house in the late afternoon. If you'd like to come pick it up, I could wait for you at five. Do you like tea?"

Silence on my end.

"If you have time, of course! You don't work when you're here too, I hope!?"

"Oh, no, no!"

"At five o'clock, then. Teresa Lucibello will give you my address."

After my thank-you and a handshake I never would have dared to hope for, I rush with an urgency and an energy worthy only of Nicola when he's overwhelmed by his never-satisfied adolescent dreams. With a few rapid movements, I push the boat into the sea and jump in, grabbing the oars in my hands like the necks of two nuns. I row with such force that in just a few minutes I see her slight figure, composedly gathered under her mantle, transform in the distance into an ionic column free-standing on the beach. If Nicola knew the fullness of the contours hidden by her clothes . . . But I steer clear of saying this to him as he walks over to me on the strand and takes hold of the boat, staring into my eyes suspiciously.

4

The woman's house, perched on a coastal cliff, was exactly like her. Not the figure that I had heard so much about by then in terms of luxury and status, but the person who emanated directly from her stride, the one only Nicola and I "felt." An example: there wasn't a trace of all of those fabled paintings talked about in town; rather, the walls were left rough and whitewashed, just like the ones in the Lucibello house. The decor was a succession of serene areas of whitewash and glass, interrupted by an ivory-colored sofa here, a table there, or by the large, light-colored ottoman, the kind that would have once sat in the middle of the ballroom in any noble palazzo in the south. That piece of furniture, as big as a king-sized bed, brought my mind back to a past buried so deep it gave me chills: ghosts of children in white, pink, and blue with black patent-leather shoes crowded laughing onto the ottoman, which in my memories was a dark-red velvet, where the joy of rolling around, or simply lying down next to one's best friend, chatting after all of those waltzes, was like nothing else.

"That piece of furniture is the only thing I held on to from my house. It was too important to me, and I managed to save it from the foreclosure auction. Yes, just as you said: it was velvet, but green, not red, and very dark, as was the norm. In the end it was so peeled—it looked like a bald, senile head—I had to put a new covering over it. And here, with all the colors and light, there was really no choice but to use a simple canvas."

How long have I been here? I ask myself. Maybe I should leave, but the voice of my "ionic column," now no longer dressed in light blue but dark green, doesn't sound at all tired, and her eyes, having shifted from the ottoman to look at me, seem frayed with the same green as her dress. Even after counting on the small table the cups of tea that I've sipped, as well as the numerous smoked cigarettes—a wake-up call not to overstay my welcome—I am unable to move.

Maybe I'd never be able to, if she didn't say: "Will you stay for dinner, Goliarda? It's only in an hour, and we could take the opportunity to look at my paintings. Forgive my vanity, but I'm so proud of them that as soon as I meet someone...But I don't keep them hanging throughout the house, they spoil if they're always in view. As with everything else, you grow used to their presence, and the paintings get offended and become sad. Even beauty can be tiring, don't you think?"

"Thank you, but I can't stay for dinner, I'm supposed to see someone. I'd be happy to take a look at your artistic treasures, though."

"How wonderful! I was afraid you weren't a fan of painting. Well then, come. I keep all of them in a big room that has the right temperature. It's ventilated and there's no humidity—plus it's far from indiscreet eyes. It's one of the reasons I love this house. In Milan my place is so small!"

On the top floor, with light steps she leads me through a full-fledged gallery, with windows facing the rocky mountain walls on one side and, on the other, the veil of a sea so clear as to appear white. There, in front of one of those luminous framed views, I have the impression that her eyes have become white, and I feel afraid, as if I were standing in front of a ghost.

"You must be tired," her voice suddenly suggests, it too a white affirmation. "Just this last painting, the crown jewel of my collection, and I'll let you go."

It was there, in that sort of a bare attic—there was nothing but paintings and a long bench from a convent refectory in the center—that I saw my first painting by Francis Bacon. I was left speechless, stone-still, almost more terrified than by the white I had thought I'd seen flood her eyes a moment before.

I don't know why, but after the usual pleasantries, we simply say goodbye, without a word about meeting again or any vague agreement for the future. Once I'm out in the open air, as if waking up from a spell, everything seems beautiful, vital, though also a bit ordinary: the long goat path at that point looking over the precipice, the large carob trees shielding it on the left side toward the mountain, a pomegranate tree with its ruby-red paper flowers already in bloom, two or three fig trees casting large shadows—everything up to the Saracen tower, round and delicate like the exquisite shapes of the cakes Giacomino makes for Easter.

After the tower, three little barefoot girls with hay-blond hair come walking in my direction. They move with an athletic stride, so different from the girls of our day— mine and the woman's, I mean—already suggesting something absolutely free of modesty. I recognize the group: two of them are the Caetani girls, an old family, once the owners of the entire southern side of the town, known as La Sponda—or the Shore—and now fallen, if not into poverty, at least into tight circumstances due to a classic case of a gambling father.

The well-built Raimonda, who would be fat if her flesh didn't have in it that aristocratic plasticity—a Maillol, I think, or a Picasso from his monumental period—shoots toward me, followed by her slender nymphet of a sister, with her big, scared squirrel's eyes, and by a country girl employed by the family.

Raimonda addresses me in her typically harsh tone: "What are you doing here? You do realize that you're walking on our property?"

"I'm just coming from seeing Princess Beneventano."

"Ah!" she exclaims, opening a pretty mouth, somewhere between a proper young lady's and an urchin's. She roams around like a rowdy boy, and, from what I've gathered from another local, Filiberto, she often gets into fistfights with her male friends, the sons of fishermen, and by all accounts she wins. "All right, in that case. Good for you! I've never been able to go into that house. Is it a dream like they say it is?"

I start to push a bit to make my way along the path, which is so narrow I can't go forward unless she gets out of the way.

She moves aside so respectfully I almost laugh. If I had time, I'd stay and talk to them. But I'm in too much of a hurry, not wanting to spoil with other impressions everything I've just come to know which is still fluttering within me—the house, the invitation to dinner, and most importantly, the discovery that her eyes can change color.

However, at night, as I get into bed and think back on the day, I consider how she didn't suggest another time to meet, let alone encourage me to show my face again.

Would you look at that, I think, somewhat disappointed despite the great conquest that fate has handed me: after months, I was finally getting somewhere, and now I'm back where I started. As much as I can, I console myself with the thought that life itself takes that course, it always starts over from the beginning.

5

The next morning, after some perfect analysis or synthesis that has taken place without my knowing it (the logical mystery of that general rehearsal for death we call sleep), I wake up feeling serene, as if I'd honorably brought a task to conclusion. With lightness in every limb, I head out into those toy streets, pinkish from the slanting rays of a benevolent, newborn sun, and I duck into Giacomino's small café. With the gestures of an ancient god, the great pastry chef carries the fruits of his alchemy over which he and his sorcerer's apprentices have labored down in their underground chamber scented with baking powder and cinnamon. Without hesitation, I order rum babas in abundance and cappuccinos by the gallon.

Head down, I move toward the first table that my hungry mind is able to spot, but I find it's already taken. I'm about to turn toward the one farther in the back—there were only three tables then, before Giacomino found the solution of extending the seating area outside into his orange grove—when the voice I now know well rings out sharp and clear after a good night's sleep, like the light seeping in joyously from the windows.

"Come, Goliarda, by all means sit here. I don't know if you're the same way, but I prefer not to have breakfast by myself in the morning."

The plate in my hand carrying the pastries does not tremble even slightly, a sign that I knew I'd meet her.

"Oh, thank you. I also hate having breakfast alone."

I sit down and look at her. The way she is now, in the morning, she's even more beautiful. Forgetting my babas, I can't help but stare at her in silence, completely struck by this morning splendor sitting before me.

"Because both of us grew up in a large family," I say breezily. "Isn't that why?"

"It's no longer fashionable to say so," she answers in the same way, "but large families were a magnificent thing. Sometimes I feel like all of this constant talk of the destruction of the family as progress isn't anything but a way for the powerful to convince the poor not to have children. Haven't you noticed how the rich go on having as many kids as they like? Nowadays children are a luxury, and with the slogan 'down with the family' they console the poor things who wouldn't have the means to raise any in the first place."

For a second, it sounds to me like a classic reactionary's argument, as people said back then, and I start to fear I'll see her image crumble in front of me in the usual disappointment of discovering that she is a Fascist or a monarchist. But, as if sensing my fear, she hurries to say: "Oh, don't worry! I'm not a right-winger, it's just that I was fortunate enough to have a very intelligent father. Sure, my family weren't revolutionaries, but they were enlightened enough. You see, when I think of my ancestors, I get the feeling that our lineage is a perfect synthesis of Italy. On one side, a procession of military men, a few bishops; on the other—the one I belong to more—members of the Carbonari, of the Garibaldini, Freemasons. Freemasonry had many merits, even if now it's become a bit...muddled. On one side men like Beccaria, Murri, Pirandello, on the other the great literary line going from Manzoni all the way to Vasco Pratolini today...Don't you find that Pratolini, whom the Communists like so much, is a bit—how to put it?—churchy, or that he's religiously devoted to the exaltation and conservation of all of the 'good virtues'? But listen to me gabbing, I'll ruin your breakfast. It's one of my bad qualities, everyone at home criticizes me for it. It's just that in the morning my mind is so awake and full of energy that—"

"No, no, what you're saying is really interesting. I agree with you completely!"

I'm about to add that my apparent embarrassment was only due to the discovery that she is not just beautiful, but intelligent too. Luckily, I stop myself in time, reflecting on how all of us—myself included, even if I think I'm so beyond clichés—are stuffed like a Christmas turkey with prejudices: beautiful, therefore dumb.

"When you make that face—I noticed it yesterday too during our trip through the mysteries of modern painting—you look like a little girl, Goliarda."

"I've thought a lot about those paintings, and was wondering why there are only contemporary artists in your collection. Perhaps you don't like classical painting . . ."

"I like it very much, actually! As a girl I dreamed of becoming like one of Botticelli's women."

"And you weren't wrong. At times there's something about you, especially in your walk . . . I, on the other hand, dreamed of becoming like one of Renoir's young gals, sitting at the bar with a glass in front of me."

She laughs. Encouraged, I add, "I even got my hands on a copy of that painting and hung it on the wall over my bed, convinced that over time it would shape me in its image."

Her laugh becomes higher and more melodious. It grows with the sun, that laugh. I keep talking just to hear more of it. "A waste of time, I know. I never managed to get rid of this gait of mine, like something between a deckhand and a mobster, as Marilú pointed out to me."

"Is Marilú your sister?"

"Oh no, just a close friend."

"You have a lot of friends, don't you? I heard as much from Pierpaolo Piccinato, who said he's known you since '47."

"Yes, they're the most precious things I have, just as your collection of paintings is for you. And Marilú Karteny is really the crown jewel of them all... But do you know Pierpaolo? Wasn't he in Paris?"

"All predestined individuals end up here in Positano. Paolo is truly an original. He refused to work as an architect, to him that profession does nothing but contribute to the ongoing massacre of our European continent. He has an extraordinary voice and ear. When I asked him, 'Couldn't you have been a singer?'—maybe you already know that he's close to Brassens—he replied: 'Oh, it's all the same! It's a slightly less conscious way of taking part in our global crime against nature.' But why talk about crimes... Now he makes magnificent flutes for a living, he learned the technique in Greece, and he even does an occasional mosaic."

Why, while speaking of Pierpaolo, as the sun rises slowly to cover her, has her voice become so sad? I want to hear her talk about herself, and I interrupt her, maybe even too abruptly.

"Oh, I love Pierpaolo, but why don't you tell me more about yourself, about your childhood?"

Even more sadly, she replies, "I'm really interested in you, too, Goliarda. For months I'd been trying to meet you through our mutual friends. But, as we all know, friends are like brothers or sisters, they're so jealous of new arrivals."

"It's a good thing I had the excuse of the sun cream to overcome my shyness, seeing as you're also shy..."

"I've never had girlfriends. I had two sisters, yes. But sisters...Listen, now I truly need my morning sea. Should we act as if our shyness didn't exist and see each other again? The funny thing is that I don't feel this self-consciousness with men. I'm almost *too* forward with them...Who knows what it means!"

She's suddenly so agitated, nearly stuttering, that I'm left speechless. Now my shyness has returned, blocking me from saying something friendly, reassuring, leaving me to witness powerlessly as she stands up and makes it almost to the exit before I manage to utter a word. As it so happens, I'm generally not shy with men or with women, so why this deranged feeling of uncertainty every time I see her? Is she too beautiful? Too full of passion? It's fear, I conclude in a flash, remembering the near whiteness that gleamed from her eyes yesterday in front of the window. Am I afraid for her, or for myself? No, it's for her that I fear something. As if she's been called back by my ruminations, she turns around rapidly and shouts, "So you'll come by again for tea one of these afternoons?"

"Of course!"

With a big smile, she says, "In that case come by whenever you like after five o'clock and you'll find me waiting for you. I always spend the late afternoon at home."

The smile on her full lips, as it reveals a corolla of almost too white teeth, contradicts her eyes. This woman really is strange when she smiles. There, now I see what it is: she only smiles with her lips, while her eyes always stay sad—in fact, the more her lips part, the deeper and darker her pupils become.

Giacomino, who that very moment is coming out from his cavern-confectionery, looks at me, complicit and amused. The blue beret he always wears, lightly dusted with flour, makes his face look so pale and his usually blue eyes so silver—a kind of mocking color?—that my fear from before turns into a chill inside of me. The suspicion that this town is inhabited by ghosts comes over me again, and even the joking voice of my laboring friend is no help: "Hey, you finally met her. I'm glad, she's a classy woman, our Erica, not like those tomboys—no offense—that you're always hanging around with!"

What does it mean? I ask myself as I fly down the usual enchanted steps, which resound softly, caressing the ears with an unearthly melody. I warm up by running under the sun, and having reached the docks, I throw myself panting onto the pebbly shore. I understand why legend has it that precisely there in front of me, Odysseus encountered the sirens. It's simple: that song was nothing but the silence I'm listening to now, the silence of spheres circling around each other in space, the silence of the noiseless, serene wandering of the souls of the dead through the infinite field of nonbeing.

My "religious" side, which, despite the number of times I was berated by my parents, used to drive me as a child to go pray in front of the knotty Saracen olive tree, to me a god as old and knowing as the world, or before any rock whose shape suggested to me the image of a secular angel or seagull, is again rising up in me, burning with the same intensity as the pebbles beneath me.

This town will be the end of me. It's too haunting a mystery, I must leave and never set foot in it again. There, those long unfurling curtains of rocks, now rosy in the calm April morning, gathering the small bay and my body in a dizzying embrace, they are just one of the countless, magnificent forms that the devil, that master shape-shifter, knows to take when he wants to pull you down. I need to get out of here. With urgent telegrams from Rome—back then there were only two or three phones in Positano— Luchino Visconti has even called me away: "What are you doing wasting your time in that town, Goliarda? I'm disappointed in you. Someone your age should be here in the city, taking action."

· 6 ·

I must have fallen asleep for only a minute, but I'm covered in sweat from my feelings of guilt after being called back to the world. I open my eyes in alarm at the light noise of pebbles, like the sound of a woman's hand digging in a bowl of sugared candies, while a voice falls silvery from above, fragrant with seaweed.

"What are you doing here? It's dangerous to fall asleep under the April sun. And look, it's all cloudy now. A storm is going to break soon . . . Teresa, why in the world didn't you wake the woman? On your feet, up you go, and put on this pullover. Forgive me if it's none of my business, but you're drenched in sweat."

The voice of my devil disguised as an angel reprimands me, though sweetly, and thinking that it's really a shame that she doesn't have children, I say abruptly, "It's just that I need to leave today!"

Now she's laughing. "But how, when you're lying there half-naked and with no suitcases? Plus, the boat comes in the afternoon."

"Thing is, I thought I'd go up to pack my bags and take the noon coach. But I fell asleep."

"Don't worry, Princess," says Teresa. "It's not the first time Iuzza has fallen asleep by the boats . . . Nothing gets to her, not the sun and not the cold either."

By now Teresa calls me the same way my friends do, she's quick to pick up on things. She walks over to me, takes me by the hand, and helps me up, proud to show how much familiarity there is between us—an entire shared history.

"Just think, last year she went swimming up through December, just like my boy Nicola. There's no way of stopping her."

"All right!" Erica resumes quickly. "That doesn't change the fact that this is all pretty dangerous. Sorry, what did you call her? Iuzza? What kind of name is that?"

"Sicilian!" I answer proudly, though I couldn't say why. It's a fault of mine: as soon as two women focus their attention on me, I feel flat-out happy and satisfied.

"All right, all right," she repeats even more quickly. "'Iuzza' is lovely, can I also call you that? Come on, did you feel those drops? Don't forget my boat, Teresa."

"Nicola, take care of the skiff!"

With that command of Teresa's, the beach is suddenly turned into a ship's deck, its crew bustling to prepare for the storm. Everyone is running: some gather the few beach chairs and close the umbrellas while others head toward the sea to dock the larger boats and drag the smaller ones ashore. From the lions' stairway, waiters and lifeguards run in our direction to give them a hand. I feel myself being pulled upward, as a black wall of clouds moves in from off-shore toward the small bay. Or is "she" the one who, with a vigorous hand, is guiding me now? In a few seconds we've climbed the large steps. But not in time to take refuge in a café or shop.

"We didn't make it!" my princess sighs, oddly joyous as water pours onto us, thundering down as if an entire ocean were spilling onto the beach, the steps, the small esplanade, all of it the calm stage of a miniature theater until only a few moments earlier.

"We didn't make it," she says again, even happier than the first time, adding: "We might as well enjoy the show."

I turn to look at her, because her hand has let go of mine. I watch as her face slowly circles back to look at the sea, which has now risen to become an actual barricade of foam, blocking out the horizon and even part of the beach itself.

"It's magnificent!"

Her voice sounds as if it is shouting across a distance, and yet she's there next to me, her beautiful head, her neck, and her chest seemingly molded by the furious rain, her long hair now streaming, her widened eyes taking in the powerful, rhythmic succession of waves. The figurehead of a pirate ship, it's impossible not to think; and while I can't say *You are magnificent*, I make do with saying near to her: "Yes, it is magnificent."

"There's nothing left for us to do but to go home, my little... Iuzza, right? Come on, be brave now!"

She is right to say that, because I never would have thought I'd have to face the whitewater rapids that the narrow stairways of Positano turn into when it rains. Head down, following her shoulder which steadily grows taller and sturdier as the rain picks up, apparently nourished by that deluge, I face the waves of water crashing against our climbing bodies. I follow her bare, firm feet on the slippery and glimmering flagstones, but mine are clumsy in soaked espadrilles and struggle to keep up with those prehensile toes. I kick the shoes off as best I can, finally understanding what the local custom of going barefoot is all about, and I yell happily with a feeling of liberation rising from below and flooding my entire body, which has suddenly gone back to being a child's.

"Now go, quick, into the shower, or tomorrow you won't feel so happy about all this splashing around."

When I emerge from the bathroom, reentering that large hallway barely lit by the windows facing the mountain ridge, it is so quiet that I stop, nearly panic-stricken. There's no one here, I think, I've fallen into the hands of this woman who just a little while ago unleashed a storm (roaring thunder shook the house when we came in), and now she has calmed everything again—maybe, having achieved her goal of bringing me here, she has set free the sirens who serve her. *And if she's a murderer?* I wonder, trying to joke with myself, partly to quiet my heart which has started beating frantically in the silence. But where do I go? The house is enormous, one door after the next trail after me on the left. On the right I see nothing but dark slits, now that the mountain has disappeared.

"No, don't go down the hallway! Take the stairs."

These instructions come just in time, because straight in front of me on the right, at a slight bend in the hallway, a steep stairway leads downward with no railing. Today is not the day the murderer has chosen to strike, I think. The fun in this kind of activity is all in spying on one's victim and plotting, everyone knows that.

"What does everyone know? Are you talking to yourself? I made a nice fire and hot tea... Here you go. This is my bunker for the winter, or for when there are downpours. It gets too noisy upstairs."

As a matter of fact, another bomb can be heard dropping above, but far away now, a mere echo of the fury from before.

"Or when the sirocco's blowing, since it doesn't reach down here... I had it made from the old cistern which was no longer used. I had to close the mouth of the well, of course. Look, this is where they'd drop the bucket. But there wasn't any water anymore. Better in the end, wouldn't you say?"

She doesn't wait for an answer, but who couldn't like that nook completely covered in silk, with two soft, red, velvet loveseats near the fire and a thick white carpet underfoot, like the fleece of an ancient animal.

"Also, it's here that I hold on to all of my fondest memories...No, not tangible mementos like photographs and other objects...I come here when I want to remember. Actually, I'd appreciate it if you didn't tell any of our mutual friends about this room. I've never brought any of them here. You can close off those stairs you took to come down. I would bet even Lorenzo with all his curiosity and imagination couldn't notice them when they're covered up. Oh, that Lorenzo! He wouldn't stop talking about you, but he never wanted to bring you here...In fact, I've never even met his sister, Lietta. They say she's very smart, and a real riot."

"Oh, she definitely is!" I blurt out, relieved by that reference to living people after all the ghosts that, in spite of myself, I've felt hovering around from the moment I stepped foot in this room, so unimaginable after the vast, bright spaces upstairs.

"Do you know her well?"

"Oh, do I! Since '47. If you'd like, I'll bring her here myself."

"No, that's not the reason I mentioned her. They, my friends, try to isolate me, but I don't blame them. That's the way friendship is, a little like love...possessive, I mean. But fortunately, I only put up with them when I want to. As you can see in your own case, when I considered meeting you indispensable, I did it."

As she utters these last words, she half closes her large eyes, stretched toward her temples. Now they stare at me again, silvery like sharpened knife blades. That gaze is too much for me. I go back to looking at my surroundings, as the panic I felt before while groping through that dark, un-natural silence takes hold of me once again.

"You don't happen to suffer from claustrophobia, do you? Don't worry, behind that curtain, on your right, there is a window looking out onto the base of the mountain. Do you want to see? I had it cut out in the wall of the well. Sure, I could have put it on the side facing the sea, behind me here, but then the soundproofing effect would have been lost. And then, by digging an opening in these old walls—just think, they were a meter and a half thick—I not only can have light when I want, but the rest of the house is in-sulated from moisture and humidity, too."

Through the wide-opened window, in an aquatic light, I see one of the many slopes of Positano rising steeply just two meters in front of me. It's a persistent pink, even in that funerary chapel half-light. The openings in the mountain (or the wounds, as Giacomino calls them) are still visible, and as I look up, it takes the full extension and flexibility of my neck to glimpse a strip of faded blue sky above. Maybe it has stopped raining, I think, when suddenly a scattering of drops falls like confetti on my outstretched face.

"You separated the whole house from the side of the mountain."

"Oh yes, we had to. You can't imagine how damp it would get before."

"The work of a true architect."

"Ah, I wouldn't want to take all of the credit. The master craftsmen in this town are extraordinary. You only need to guide them. Too bad that they're disappearing, the younger generations don't want anything to do with carrying on that work. They still know how to build vaults the ancient way, just like the ones in Palazzo Murat. All of us old-time *positanesi* had our houses built or reconstructed by them. But by now the barbarians have discovered our town."

"The barbarians?"

"The northern and southern bourgeoisie who've started flocking here ever since they widened the road. To get to the Amalfi Coast, we would usually come with a coach or a taxi from the Naples train station; and only by carriage while my father was around, just like my grandfather before him. It was so lovely coming here by carriage... Frightening and exhilarating, as it must have been in Stendhal's time. But now the bourgeois barbarians have found us out, and unfortunately, despite the ban placed by the owner of the Hotel Sirenuse, who's also the mayor—we owe it to him if Positano hasn't been completely ruined like Sorrento— they're starting to entrust the construction of their homes to firms in Milan that can throw them together in no time. They're exactly like the old ones on the outside, but don't even get me started on the inside—paper walls, like boxes of noise. But I'm probably boring you."

While saying this, she has shut the window, drawn the heavy curtain, and, after rummaging gracefully through the mammoth pieces of firewood, sat back down in the velvet, flaming-red chair. Now she's quiet, looking at her hands, which rest one on top of the other. She is waiting. Those hands are giving me an order. Am I supposed to say something, or sit in silence?

"You're not saying a thing," she whispers as if to herself. "You observe impassively while quietly sitting there."

"Oh, sometimes I'm quiet, other times I'm a chatterbox, as my mother used to say. It depends . . ."

"Of course." She stares at me with eyes again opened wide, reflecting the vivid red of the flames.

Who carried that heavy wood down the stairs? She can't do all of those things by herself, I think. Maybe she has an army of elves seeing to everything, maybe even right now they're around us waiting for orders from their fairy queen.

It could be the knowledge that there is at least a window in that bunker, or it's the warm shower and the nice tea starting to take effect, but, for whatever reason, a feeling of relaxation comes over me and, convinced that I want nothing but to position my body more comfortably in a seat that is as welcoming as two loving arms, I doze off right there, caressed by her gaze which has gone back to being tender and maternal. It's truly a shame that she doesn't have children, but she still could have them, she's young, I have just enough time to think before falling asleep.

When I open my eyes, she's there in front of me, reading. She's wearing glasses. Those thin and long reading glasses are so funny, lost in the middle of a face with such broad features! I shut my eyes again to fight back a smile. I sit tight, enjoying the warmth and her familiar closeness. Someone has covered me with a blanket. My mother, surely. She conjured up my mother, who died years ago. My mother also wore those glasses, even when she was young.

"Oh, farsightedness and white hair—every morning I find one or two more—they go all the way back in my family."

"No way!" I exclaim with false astonishment at a fact I already knew. "In my mother's family, too, it was passed down on the maternal side."

"She died a long time ago, didn't she?"

She's lying, too. She knows everything and pretends not to. Regardless, I reply, "A very long time ago, yes, but I miss her terribly. Sometimes I see her, can even smell the scent of her body."

"The dead do come back," she says.

"Do you believe in God?"

"Yes, but in an algebraic god. Who knows, maybe it's only because, in the little studying I did, my favorite subject was math. Calculus was so fascinating to me! More thrilling than the colors and images of the great masters, or the great poems, if that's possible. I also inherited this from my family. My father, like my grandfather, was an excellent mathematician."

"But wasn't he a prince?"

"Ah yes, I know they call me 'princess' in the town, but it's all nonsense. I let them say it so as not to disappoint their thirst for kings and queens, which is rampant here around Naples. My family goes back a long way, and was very rich once—half of Sicily belonged to it—but we lost all of our titles of nobility. Sure, as my sister Fiore would say to me, shoving our genealogical tree in my face every chance she got, compare us to all of these post-Italian unification nobles...But what nonsense! All of our nobility, along with all of our land, was lost with my father's generation. It had started with my great-grandfather, squandering his money on luxuries. They had to try to make up for it by marrying rich bourgeois individuals all over the place. Take me: I'm an absurd mix of ethnicities. My grandmother was the daughter of an English shopkeeper whom my grand-father had met in London, where, like any good *palermitano*, he used to go to get his shirts. I was born in Florence, and as a little girl I'd go to Sicily. I never set foot on the island after...I'd like to, but I'm always afraid to see it again, I only know it from the family photographs. One day I'll overcome my fear—maybe it's due to all the bad things Italians on the mainland say about the place? When I do work up the cour-age to go, it will be to buy back a villa that they tell me has been left intact. My grandmother always talked to me about that place, from her watercolors too it seems like a dream house. My grandmother liked dabbling in painting, writ-ing sonnets, and singing. Amazing all the things people did without a camera to take pictures! Her watercolors, those sketches said the most. Maybe they weren't realistic, but they could make you dream...Listen, Goliarda, while you were sleeping you said the word 'murderer' several times. Were you having a dream? Oh, forgive me if you don't want to answer, but that word made me so curious."

With a frankness that surprises even me, I hear my-self reply: "It must mean I was dreaming about you. When I came out of the bathroom and you called me, I felt like I had fallen into the trap of a murderous woman, or a Circe—however you want to put it. The power of myths. They're inescapable in this town. Every rock, wall, ancient carob tree, calls them back to mind."

"'Murderer,' really?" she whispers to herself, immedi-ately adding a smile. "Well, why not? Don't we all have a bit of a murderer inside of us? Hasn't every one of us, or nearly, dreamed deep down of killing our present tormentor, beaten down by the harm that others do to us, even if unconsciously?"

"Oh, of course!" I respond, laughing in spite of myself. "If you only knew how many people I killed when I was little..."

"And why are you laughing now?"

Have I offended her? No, even her eyes are laughing for once, joining in on the joke.

"It's because of those glasses you're holding. Put them down, would you? They're so funny in your hands, and looked so out of keeping earlier with the grandeur that is your whole person."

"Oh dear!" she laughs, pushing away the small glasses on the low, shining glass table separating us. "Well, why don't we go now. They tell me that dinner is ready upstairs." Who sent her this message? Invisible elves, no doubt. "Aren't you hungry? I'm starving so much I actually have cramps. My constitution calls for a lot of food, especially when I've been outdoors or gone swimming."

My stomach is cramping, too, but how could this be? Only a moment has passed since I gobbled down all of those sweets and tarts with the tea.

"You'll see what kind of delicious things Nunziatina has made for us. She's magic."

"Nunziatina who? Nicola and Teresa Lucibello's sister? The one who cooks for the American women?"

"Yes, Irma and Edna also take advantage of Nunziatina's talents, but I'm the one who lends her to them, as

I also do for some rich big shots who come here during high season. You see," she keeps talking as she walks up the steep stairs, "when I met Nunziatina, she—like almost everyone else in the town, for that matter—was so poor, she couldn't even afford a pair of shoes, and so I took her in to work for me. Oh, not only out of kindness: she knew how to do everything. Then, here with me and with the butler, or the house maestro as we say in Sicily, who's looked after me since I was a child, she's really become 'polished.' And so I started to let her go earn money freely, though I still pay her through the summer and the winter, naturally. I'm so happy for her, she's rich now, her children can study, which is a mistake in my opinion. But what can you do, modern times keep moving along, with all of the silent disasters that we already know—there's no point in fighting the tides of history. The only thing that matters to me is that she's happy and that she stays close to me. Oh, and that's also not out of altruism: when she's happy, she's a better cook."

Once we're outside of the opening at the top of the stairs, my friend shuts the thick trapdoor with a swipe of her bare foot, like the movement of a ballerina or a graceful monkey. Now the floor of the hallway looks so uniform—it's all wood—that I'd be surprised if even a specialized detective could find that hidden passage. I'm dying to know how she'll open it again, maybe there's a lever or a button, but I'm too hungry to inquire about other mysteries, and, setting them aside, I follow her.

At dinner, on the small covered terrace—the rain has stopped, but it's too damp to eat in the large roof garden—we practically don't speak, or only make a bit of silly small talk, as one used to do. Older people would say that silence at the table made the food more nutritious and helped the digestion. But those were humbler, peasant times, I think to myself, while I savor all of those delicacies that would have been unimaginable when she and I were little girls.

The crisp whiteness of the embroidered tablecloth becomes even brighter thanks to the candles, the glimmering crystals and maiolicas, and is further embellished by the beautiful bouquet—Nunziatina's artistic signature both in that solitary house and on the constantly crowded and noisy tables of the old democratic sorceresses or witches, who for the occasion assumed the names familiar to us of Irma and Edna.

"Ah, those two Australian women"—I thought they were American—"found their own America here in Positano—believe me, Goliarda—with their idea of opening a workshop for women from London, New York, or Sydney. These women, oppressed by their colorless, alienating work in the big cities, can come, for almost no money, for a week or fifteen days with full board, and between a swim and a stroll learn to draw, sculpt, and make mosaics. True entrepreneurs, Irma and Edna! But they do good for the town, they're not driven merely to rake in money. They help all of the poor artists who come here. Positano, as my father used to say, has always been the destination of the different, in every sense. He said that you could see Positano syndrome written on the faces of the most disparate people whom the god of travel made you run into here: a shop girl from

Milan, a doctor, a writer. In 1922—I don't remember if he
was with Alvaro or Pirandello—he saw for the second time
two lesbian singers he'd listened to by chance in a Berlin
cabaret. Only that in Berlin they presented themselves to
the audience as the daintiest, most feminine twins, while
here in Positano they revealed themselves for who they
were, walking hand in hand and exchanging quick kisses,
concealed behind some corner or by the dark of the moon-
less summer nights. The town wasn't lit back then, and it
seems the feeling of freedom was even more absolute. But
going back to Irma and Edna, they also pay poor artists as
teachers. They've saved so many from going hungry. Even
our friend Pierpaolo just yesterday was hired as a mosaics
teacher. It seems like he's really talented. I'd like to have
him make one in the house, that way he can top off his salary. Will you help me choose a good wall for it?"

How could she possibly know all of these things? She
was never seen out in the town. In her house, I'd learned,
there was no telephone. Probably she had, in addition to
the invisible helpers cleaning and attending to her, a whole
other legion of informant elves, keeping her up to date on
the goings-on in town. *And there must be a pianist elf too*, I
say to myself, surprised to hear suddenly a Chopin sonata
that, after two or three exercises to check the sound, has
filled the silence that always falls over nature and people's
spirits following a storm.

"Who's playing? It sounds like an angel!" I say with my
heart thrown into a frenzy by the delicate virtuosity of fingers I feel I can actually see.

"It's Kempf. We don't only have poor artists in Positano, you know," she answers, jokingly. That chiming, sweet song must have gotten to her too, I can hear it in her slightly cracked voice.

"Two years ago, he came to live right near here. Oh, in a manner of speaking—you know how Positano is, near as the crow flies, but always with a few sheer drops in the middle. That character chose such a high and solitary cliff that I can still remember how crazy it was for them to get his piano up there. The whole town watched that morning. For the last stretch they needed a crane. It was so scary to see that old, precious object swinging by the sharp rocks. Everyone stretched out their necks to follow its journey upward, their hearts in their mouths. And when the piano disappeared behind the wall of the old abandoned church he had bought, no one moved. It's unbelievable, but everyone waited, I think for an hour or two. Did it make it safe and sound? No one could say! When suddenly, just like tonight, the maestro, out of happiness for the successful undertaking, or maybe to thank everyone for waiting, after two or three arpeggios sent hurtling down from the heights a wild hymn of joy. I was so filled with emotion that now I can't even remember the piece he played for us. Since that morning, every night after dinner he offers to the cliffs and to their inhabitants one or two pieces, like an impromptu concert. However, no matter the applause, he never gives an encore."

I don't know if I've fallen under the spell of the music, or if it's the silence after the storm which, like those first notes, has abruptly settled around us again—that meta-physical silence of the Amalfi Coast—but I end up starting to talk about myself, telling her everything in that un-stoppable outpouring of friendship that can happen only once, maybe twice, in life, and is capable of sweeping away all fear of not being understood, all concern over how you might come across to the other person.

By the end, we somehow made our way from the small terrace to the large living room, a place familiar to me, nothing but glass and white walls. We sank into the couch close to one another, holding glasses of whiskey on ice. She was staring intensely at the cubes, small icebergs in a calm sea of amber. Having let out everything, I was beginning to feel uncomfortable, as always happens in such instances. I had told her all of it, even things that I would have been ashamed to share with my man. I didn't dare look at her, despite the fact that something like a caress was fluttering around me—a deceitful caress, most likely.

When she finally looked up at me with her large, sad eyes, she waited awhile before speaking. "What you told me, Goliarda, calls for a promise on my part. Or better yet, a duty."

A duty? I think, bewildered.

"Yes, the duty to love you, and more than just as the chance friend I thought I had made. Poor little girl! Now I feel like I know that Iuzza who was still such a mystery to me. But I know how to reciprocate this trust. For a few years I've been avoiding real friendship, real involvement, even in love, and that's how this need, which I'd struggled to suppress, drove me to try to find you. There's no escaping it. Don't feel guilty. While you were speaking I realized why you had intrigued me so much. Thank you."

That thank-you washes away all of the feelings of guilt that had been weighing on me (even atheists need confession): having hated my father unfairly, having mistreated my mother, having killed a German soldier during the Resistance—for political reasons, of course, but murder all the same.

I apologize for the digression—unfortunately, not poetically humorous à la *Tristram Shandy*—and should focus back on my "sweet lady," as I called her to myself from that evening on, copying Teresa. Right, because despite her sweetness, and her barely whispered *Thank you*, there had been something distancing her, or rather, something that was so much her own—dignified and pained at the same time—that, despite her willingness to give herself generously to another, made her seem far away, just like the smile currently wavering on those perfect yet overly large lips, her high forehead, her sculpted nose which almost looked like a masculine feature placed by accident in the middle of cheeks, weightless hair, and a complexion that were all too exquisitely feminine.

"I see that you're tired, you're staring at me without seeing me. I'm going to take the liberty of suggesting you sleep here—it's almost midnight. This town might be the only place in Italy where a woman can walk around at night without anyone bothering her. I've never understood if it's to hold on to the vacationers they make their money off of, or just out of great civility. But either way, I still wouldn't like to think of you going down all of those steps alone in the dark."

"Okay, I'll stay. Not out of fear of the dark, but I'm so tired that just the thought of walking is making me feel seasick."

"Off you go to bed then. I'll put you in the most beautiful room in the house. It was intended to be for my youngest sister, but she almost never comes."

"Why not?"

"She got married, as is only right. She already has two little girls—the lucky woman—and a husband who travels all the time. It's just the way she dreamed, she also loves traveling more than anything. I miss Olivia so much, she's the only one I have left . . . Here we are, do you like the little room? Or is it too childish for you? I see that your curiosity is waking you up. We can talk about it tomorrow with the sun. Sunlight eases the pain a bit, at least enough to make it bearable. Speaking of the sun, you'll see when you wake up what kind of view awaits you. Promise that as soon as you wake up, you'll go on the terrace behind the curtains here. It's the most beautiful view in the whole house. Good night then, see you tomorrow. Sweet dreams."

Imagine that, I think to myself as I drift into sleep, she still says "Sweet dreams" as we used to say at my house. She really is old-fashioned, this woman, but with an old-fashionedness that's so distantly ancient she sometimes seems ultramodern—I think—just like Botticelli's Venus. Now that's whom she resembles. Feeling somewhat embarrassed for this unoriginal comparison—extremely common, at least since Proust popularized the painter—I fall asleep, excusing myself for having troubled that author with the essence of one of his own thoughts: that all of life's flavor can be found even in the most trivial verse of a song.

· 8 ·

The next morning, obeying her enticing command as if it had come from a goddess—and trying at the same time to laugh at my childish side always starved of fairy tales—I push open the heavy, dark curtains and then the light muslin drapes tinted gold by the sunrise. The French doors of crisp glass open onto a terrace completely covered in red flowers that have fallen from a bougainvillea. My bare feet slide happily on the terra-cotta floor. I'll stop wearing shoes, too, I think with conviction, even if it'll make me come across as a real *positanese* snob like her.

Why did I wait so long to make this decision? It's the fault of all that socialist neorealism, insists my mind as it puts down my senses for having grown rusty from ideology, despite the joy now pervading me in front of that glossy postcard of sky and sea. My imagination has been constricted by iron boots—or has it been the tight cloth they would use to bind the feet of Chinese women? I'll tear that cloth into a thousand pieces. I don't care if I'm as banal as that joyful song to life running from the heights of Praiano, the first to bask in the sun's rays on my left, to Punta Campanella, still immersed in a crisp predawn and lingering in the mythic embrace that joins it nightly with Capri.

I am so excited to have discovered this feeling of pleasure that I almost don't hear the shy voice behind me, speaking in an Italianized Positano dialect: "We received a message about a phone call for you from Rome. The princess says you need to go right away to the post office in Piazzetta dei Mulini, but to please come back for breakfast if you'd like."

It's Nunziatina's voice. I'm rather annoyed with this news—they're calling me back to my duties as a socially engaged filmmaker. After asking the messenger to tell the princess that I'll be sure to come back, I rush down to the piazza and to the bare and dusty closet that is the post office, with the perpetually broken glass in its front door, and the pungent smell of horses (and there were many of them then) standing night and day with their wobbly, worm-eaten carriages, waiting patiently in a line for sojourners.

I stop in to wait for the call from Rome. In that isolated village, like a frontier outpost, there was only one phone

booth and hardly ever a mailman. I remember how difficult it was to use the telephone or to get stamps. Whenever
you needed them, you'd find the place closed, no matter
the time of day, with a handwritten sign hanging outside
saying CLOSED FOR SORTING. Sorting—how I had laughed
with Rinaldo, Maselli's assistant director, about that word
which implied a crazy amount of postal traffic in a little
town where people hardly ever received any mail. Rinaldo
had told me how the barber next door was also nearly always closed, with a nice little sign reading GONE FOR URGENT
FAMILY MATTERS. BE BACK SHORTLY.

"I fell for it the first morning," Rinaldo explained,
"and I waited a good hour before making up my mind to
ask someone. When I did, the answer was 'Go look for him,
he must be at the bar playing cards or on the beach.' And so
every time I needed the guy, I'd go out to catch him. Once I
found him taking in the sun on Fornillo Beach, and Iuzza,
I can't tell you how hard it was to convince him to go up to
the shop to give me a shave: 'But why today of all days, sir?
Won't tomorrow be just as good?'"

"Signora, the telephone. It's Rome!"

"Rome" is screaming at me so I can hear him across
that antediluvian telephone. But instead of *Come, Iuzza,
you have to get back to work*, he tells me that I can stay here
longer. I walk out feeling so happy I could hug the horse
and then the driver staring at me languidly a few feet away,
if he weren't so high up on his seat.

"Do you want the carriage, Signorina?"

"Absolutely. If you can wait, I'll get some money from my place. I left in a hurry."

"Tomorrow is just as good. Or the day after tomorrow, next year, doesn't matter! Climb in."

True—back then in Positano you could pay on credit everywhere. Many actually payed after two, maybe three rides. The fact is, carriages have such a dreamy effect on the imagination, just like a postcard or an old sweet song, and this one has a horse to whom only Chagall could do justice. He's extremely old, but with sturdy haunches, a coat slightly faded by the years, and a wise and distant gaze. He reminds me of a certain beautifully tall and robust old man, his chest covered in salt-and-pepper hair and his silvery mane forever flittering over his large, distracted eyes. At eight o'clock every morning this man walks up and down the beach for at least half an hour before he takes a dive. Then, with vigorous strokes, he swims far enough out to send anyone who happens to be watching him into a panic. Lucibello always laughs when he tells me about this nobleman from the north; he comes to Positano all the time, but he's only ever seen in the morning and at sunset for his respective walks and swims. "He was the most beautiful man in Positano"—with this last word, Lucibello means *the world*—"and he's had gorgeous women, and the most beautiful villa in town." "What does he do?" "Anyone's guess! They say he spends all his time reading..."

"We've arrived. Here's your place... Thank you. Any time, now."

How did he know where I was headed? I wonder as I get out right in front of Erica's house. They even know where I spent the night. They know everything about everyone. But I know how hard it is to be trusted with any truly intimate knowledge!

Is their way of not commenting, of not acting surprised by anything, just a hotel staff's discretion, or is it simply another manifestation of this town's spirit? A timeless spirit; or rather, one set in a different time than the rest of the world, marked not by hours but by the primary emotions of our body—because once those emotions are reawakened by all of those steps, and by the silence, the colors, and the smells, they get the upper hand over our systematic way of thinking. Either way, that coachman was spot-on.

As soon as I walk into the cool air smelling faintly of sugared almonds—like a nuns' convent?—I feel at home. And when I see her in a dressing gown, demure and straight-fitting like the peplos worn by her Hellenic sisters, I feel an urge to hug her, but I don't. Instead I let out my emotions by running to the table, which looks set for Christmas lunch, exclaiming, "I'm starving!"

She smiles. "Oh! Me too, but I preferred to wait for you. Thank you for coming back, eating breakfast alone is so sad."

Alone, her? I think as I butter my bread. How could it be? I look up at her face, at the chasteness in her complexion and her features, from her hair to her eyes to the soft pink of her lips. It leads me to think that maybe she is frigid, and frigid women actually need affection a hundred times more than the outwardly passionate ones. In fact, looking at her closely in that full light, my masculine side picks up something that had escaped me: there's no sex appeal in her charm, not the kind we had been taught by the atomic bomb in a bikini, Rita Hayworth, a mix of voluptuous and animal attraction that many women possess, even ones far less beautiful than she is.

I am about to ask her something when I remember that "one doesn't speak during meals." Only when we've finished breakfast do I recall the urgent impulse I'd felt, but I no longer remember my question. So much the better. I feel so peaceful that just the idea of thinking methodically feels as loathsome as any test taken in class long ago.

"Do you need to go back to Rome?"

"Oh no, my boss and companion understood that I'm doing well here. And since I wasn't indispensable, he's let me off the hook."

"Really? He's not at all jealous?"

"Who knows! Maybe I'm a jealous person, too, but respect for the other person's wishes comes before everything else, and it's the same way for him. We've always lived liked that."

"Then, if you won't be offended . . . I wanted to ask you . . . Sorry, I don't know if you're rich."

"Oh no, but we get by."

"Right, great then. Wouldn't you like to stay with me for the rest of the time you can spend here? I would love it, and you could save some money. The hotels are expensive in this town."

"How lovely!" I hear myself say immediately, without even feeling surprised for her directness. "That way I can come back another time with the money I save!"

"So you accept?"

"Of course!"

"You really are the best!"

"Oh, I have no problem receiving a gift, nor giving one when I can."

"What you say strikes me as very interesting—about gifts, I mean. I'd like to explore this thought further with you, it's more important than it seems. I, for instance, know how to give, but I have trouble receiving, and I feel that this comes from a mean trait hidden in some dark corner inside of me. But now we can't miss out on such a gorgeous sun. There's one other thing that I hope you won't mind me asking of you . . . I need to be alone when I go to the sea. Really, even in the city I need to have the mornings all to myself . . . Would you be upset if after breakfast we parted ways until, say, tea time? I don't eat lunch, I only bring some fruit on the boat. Then, if you'd like . . ."

"Oh, but that's perfect! To tell you the truth, I was starting to regret accepting your hospitality because I was afraid of having to be tied at the hip, day and night, to someone else. Even with Citto Maselli I'm that way. But why am I trying to explain myself, I see that you understand."

"Your boyfriend is named Citto?"

"A term of endearment. His real name is Francesco."

"Ah, I see!" Relieved—just as I am—she laughs, happy to know that she can have me here with her but not always buzzing around her like a fly.

I also laugh. "No friendship or love can withstand being together too much."

"That's it, you took the words right out of my mouth. Until five o'clock, then, if you don't have anything else to do at that time. Nunziatina will give you the keys to the house. And enjoy your swim."

I don't know if she has already gone out or if she's still in her room, I don't know anything, but I rush outside, carried away with the joy of getting out of that house—even the most beautiful houses, just like people, can become insufferable if one doesn't get away sometimes. I fly down steps and stairways that one moment are in the shade of white and pinkish walls, fresh after the recent rain, and the next are plunged in the green of the carobs intertwining with jasmine trees, or in the thick, dazzling emerald of the orange groves: one garden after the next, drystone walls alternating with archways flaunting supple baroque curves or with the outer enclosures of villas whirling in countless flourishes.

I only stop when my hands can touch the powerful back of one of the lions. Giacomino's father gives me a nod of recognition, but for the moment he can't talk to me: he has a customer. The tall customer has shoulder blades that poke out slightly as if he were about to sprint—a swimmer's shoulders—and he's talking his head off. It's Filiberto, the sweet old man who's the former Italian champion of the crawl. He's since been degraded (or elevated?) to the status of the Oblomov of the Amalfi Coast. With his athlete's body, just barely swelled from lack of training, and his still-full head of reddish-white curls, he exhibits all the gestures and dignity of a naval commander who has accidently washed up in this town with no port and no ships.

But the way he tells it, he's never had anything to do with ships or sailing. "Me? A sailor? God forbid, Signorina. I've always suffered from terrible seasickness. I can only swim, and when I was young I even preferred the pool to the sea."

He's also the descendant of an old, fallen family. Living for years in an enormous, half-caved-in house with almost no furniture, he spends all his time sleeping and dreaming, as he puts it. Most of all, he reflects endlessly on the ruin toward which the town, and the whole world, is creeping with no chance of stopping—though he does so more with melancholic detachment than sorrow. "Both the Russians and the Americans are to blame," he always comments to anyone who feels like shooting the breeze with him. He can be found sitting after midnight on the marble bench at the edge of the Piazzetta dei Leoni. The only time he loves is the night, and, after the card game with his friends, he sits there watching the sky. During these nights of intense study, he once saw a star flying in a straight line at a never-before-seen speed and height, and he insisted that it had to be something artificial, maybe some kind of unknown weapon, like what the Germans were perfecting before they lost the war, or a spaceship coming to observe us from another planet.

Who knows what could have forced him to leave his den and go talk in that sunny *piazzetta* to the old flesh-and-bone lion who's now listening to him with an unusual amount of interest—a need for cash, maybe. I'm enormously curious to know what they are saying, but I can't do anything about it; custom here prohibits approaching two people who clearly want to be left alone.

Nicola, having spotted me from afar, has already gone to get my rowboat, and he's now waiting for me impatiently. I see it clearly when I walk up to him: a burning question mark peers out from his two anxious, pitch-dark eyes.

"You know that I slept at the princess's?"

"Sure I know! Lucky you! Tell me, is the house as nice as Nunziatina says?"

"Oh yes, it's beautiful! Why don't you ever go there yourself?"

"No, I'd be too embarrassed, I've only seen the entrance. Why didn't you want to go with her to take a swim? Or did you have a late start? She just left."

"No, I wanted to go rowing, and she also . . ."

"I see, she treats you just like one of the family. She's the same way with her sister, and with her husband too when he was alive. He preferred the motorboat. She hated the thing, she told me once, and when her husband died she sold it for almost nothing to the Shark."

"The Shark?!"

"Alfonso. Hairy character, big as a house, grim face. But he's a good guy, Alfonso. You know, the one who shows the American girls around. He got famous in America— they come here with his name written down. Only now he's fallen in love. He still accompanies them, his clients, but he treats them badly. Just yesterday, Giuditta was crying her head off right there by Teresa!"

"And who's he in love with?"

"With another American girl, but such a plain one it's impossible to say why. And poor, too. Anyway, after keeping her in his hovel of a place in La Sponda, shut up there making love—you're not offended if I tell it like it is, right?—he sent her back to America, saying to her, 'If you really want me, make some money over there and send it to me. I'll get a business going with it, then I'll call you and we'll get married.' He's already bought a motorboat with her money, it seems there's a new sport he wants to learn, and he'll use it to make a living here. He's a good guy, Alfonso, but when he gets mad, and when he makes his mind up about something, oh boy! . . . He sent her away, even if it's clearly been hard on him. My dad says that he was right, that love with no money always ends up going down the toilet. What do you think? I don't see it that way, even without money I would have held on to her. Besides, who can understand a thing with these old folks? My dad says that Alfonso is right, but when he married my mom, they didn't even have eyes to cry out of, and look at them now: love each other like crazy! In the winter, when there aren't vacationers, they still kiss, and we kids are always afraid another Lucibello is going to be born. There are seven of us already!—Anyway, you're a lucky one all right!"

"Why lucky?" I ask, captivated by his adolescent dramatics caught between healthy romanticism and the cynical lessons of the real world.

"Because now you can stay under the same roof as the princess. I heard from Teresa that you canceled your room at the Sirenuse, which means that tonight you'll be going back to her place."

"Oh yes, but I hope you don't hate me for it?"

"Why should I hate you? What could you get up to with another woman?" Now he laughs, pushing my boat out onto the water. "Yeah, I know that a lot of these women hug and smooch, but kisses don't count. Have a good swim! Maybe if you say something on my behalf, I'll come see you two ... But no, what am I saying ... Got to go, listen to my dad yelling, he turns into an animal. I don't want to end the morning getting belted, not one bit! Not even for you and the princess."

I row out with my gaze fixed on my coveted destination, the two rugged and delicate slopes of Galli Island. Would I ever make it in that little boat with nothing but the strength of my arms? Halfway there, I need to pull in the oars and rest. I lie down on the bottom of the boat, sweaty and panting, my eyes turned to the sky.

I'm stretched out with my skull even quieter and emptier, if possible, than that endless expanse of blue, when a primordial voice, with no expressiveness of any kind, whispers into my ears: "Excuse me, Signorina, could I come onto the boat to rest a little? I've come too far out from the shore."

Stunned by this voice—did I fall asleep?—I jump up in such a hurry I send the boat rocking. I see a large head (abnormally large for any being that could be called human) covered in the thick black and red curls common among natives of the Coast. I immediately look down to search for his eyes, which are staring up at me pleadingly and brazenly; a damp gaze, as dark and ruddy as his mane of hair, but revealing such an indolent and benevolent expression that it only manages to frighten me more.

"What are you doing?" he says. "You'll make the boat tip over. I'm sorry, but may I or may I not get in?"

I don't respond. I'm focused entirely on looking around and trying to understand how that human or infernal being could have swum all the way out here. On one side, Praiano looks like nothing more than a minuscule eagle's nest, while Positano is a tiny altar, a nativity scene resting on the blue tablecloth of the sea; one side of Capri extends on the left, slender and intrepid as a sailing ship. No one, I think, not even a young Filiberto, could swim all the way out here.

When with growing amazement I look back in that apparition's direction, he has already jumped up into the boat with demonic agility, and now sits by the gunwale with his head down, staring at his legs so intensely that he seems to have forgotten I exist. He's panting and smiling. Once again in control, I carefully move as far away as possible from where my unannounced guest is sitting. I look for the oar, which, if required, is no small weapon. I brush aside my last tremor of fear. Now, I hope, I'll be capable of making his acquaintance, and, taking my time, I look back up at him. He's also staring at me intently, his eyes now full of sarcasm.

"Don't be scared. Just enough time to catch my breath and I'll be out of your way. What can I do, I need to swim every morning, there's nothing like exercise for my condition."

After this little speech, he turns back to stare at his legs, and I do the same. But when my eyes pass from his powerful torso, oddly smooth in comparison to his mass of hair, I see a stump that's as wrinkly as a sundried prune. I'm about to jump, I don't know if merely into the water or all the way down to the bottom, so long as I get far away. I shut my eyes a second to regain strength, and I might not ever open them again, but now his almost delicate voice— he's noticed my horror—mumbles: "It was in Russia: frostbite. But I was lucky, I could have lost both of them, and then I would've said so long to swimming. At least this way I still can enjoy going out into the blue. It took quite a toll on my workout! But I've always had a lot of drive. I amazed doctors and neighbors—the whole Coast I amazed."

I abruptly shut my mouth, making a strange noise with my lips that I've never made before: a sound like a cork popping, in this silence that keeps growing in intensity until it's unbearable.

"Well, thank you, and have a good row."

I see him crawl rapidly along the gunwale of the boat—like an enormous spider or grasshopper—and with a nervous jump (he *is* a grasshopper) throw himself into the still water that's colored such a deep blue it would seem a lacquered floor if not for the silvery tentacles tirelessly probing its dark expanse. Amid the blue and the dancing rays, I see him plod forward with an inconceivable strength in his arms. His raised head cuts straight along the water's surface, while his arms advance slowly but rhythmically in the sure cadence of the timeless sidestroke. I watch until his large head becomes a mere dot in the middle of the sea, and only when my eyes can barely follow him do I throw myself back onto the bottom of the boat, intent on making sense of what just happened—when a terrible sleepiness comes over me again.

All I do since coming to Positano is sleep, I say to myself as I wake up after God knows how long. My mouth is dry, and I have a sole desire: get back to shore and drink something. Around me, everything is exactly as it was before my encounter, a blue peacefulness.

With the bow pointed at Positano, I slowly row toward the enameled dome of the large church which almost rests on the water. What a hard time that artisan must have had trying to find a shade of blue that wouldn't pale in comparison to the color of the sea. In Praiano, on the other hand, they made a silver dome—silver was simply a way of avoiding all contrast. Above its shimmering, I see an army of clouds, with banners and warriors on horseback preparing once again to do battle.

That white armada is getting ready to attack, and in less than an hour the heavens are going to open like yesterday, I think, as I put my back into it. I don't want to end up stuck in the middle of that war of the elements which nature delights in unleashing every so often, if only to break up the tedium that even the most celestial peace can create.

I've only just left my boat with Nicola when I see large drops land on his cheeks; with his wrists he wipes them away, along with the black flop of hair constantly falling over his eyes. He's so beautiful—excited by those drops coming down thicker and thicker—and I have to struggle not to plant a kiss on his pensive forehead. After a quick goodbye, I head toward my new dwellings, the rain chasing at my heels.

At the front door, I find myself shoulder to shoulder with my hostess. Her cheeks are also wet from the rain, and with the back of her hand she wipes away blond locks that have been darkened by the water like ancient gold. Now, without any fear, I plant two or maybe more kisses on her forehead and her eyes. She doesn't say anything, but once this outburst of emotion—unexpected until a few seconds earlier—has passed, she takes my face in her hands and returns the kisses. Then, opening the door, she says playfully: "Today they didn't manage to drench us, huh, Goliarda?"

"No they didn't, but it was lovely yesterday!"

"Because we were together. It's sad on one's own, everything is."

She disappears into one of the many hallways that open up like sunrays in an entrance as vast and bright as a ballroom. In the large back window facing me, the battle of the elements is now raging at full force. Soon even the walls of our house will be shaking.

In my room, on a small table, there is fruit, a teapot, and some sandwiches. I knew it. Happy, while the elements battle outside, like a true deserter in hiding I gobble down my fill of the fine fruits and tea of peace.

I should finish reading that book *Metello* by
Pratolini, a prime example of socialist neorealism, which they'd like to make into a film in
Rome. But Rome is far away, and that all-around
hero sprawled in an armchair with the face of
Raf Vallone or Mastroianni, or God knows who,
is doing nothing for me. Sitting next to him, a
powerful, smooth torso, shining wet and slightly
wheezing, appears in the flashes of lightning. No,
it's not seated; it's as if invisible hands are resting it directly on a wrinkly, black stump.

As I stepped off my boat onto the dock, I
hoped that I'd only dreamed what had resembled
a legless Poseidon, but Nicola's question confirmed that he actually did exist in real life: "Oh,
Signorina, did you happen to see the Spider?"

"What spider?" "Beppe the Spider, the one missing a leg. In a little while the sea's going to rise and we're a bit worried... Ah, he stopped for a rest in your boat?! In that case he'll have made it to Fornillo. I need to run and bring him his crutch." Then he pointed to a crutch resting carefully against the small table under an umbrella where Teresa keeps a record of the rented boats. "We're taking up a collection to buy him a prosthetic leg. With a new leg, no one will be able to stop our little amputee, not even on land!"

Nicola laughed, and I felt ashamed for pretending to feel pity—like a typical bourgeois or "organic" intellectual—before beginning to laugh along with him. They're in the right, with their joking kind of acceptance. They still know the ancient art our peasant ancestors had of living alongside the ills that nature and men re-create ceaselessly, in every season, along with the yearly blooming of the orange and lemon trees. Sure, in August, in order not to upset the crowds of tourists, they beg their "poor wretches" not to show themselves in public too much, but in return they feed them all year, they joke around with them, welcoming them into the cafés and into their homes.

I still didn't know Beppe the Spider, but by now I do talk to Ciccillo the Cemetery, or with Caruso, the giant touched by God, and at this point I don't think anything of it when they talk to me, something I couldn't have imagined just a few years before coming to the Coast.

"You have to give him your hand, or that giant of ours will be hurt, and, even worse, he'll give that cigarette you lent him back to you. Thing is, he's convinced he's a

Casanova, he lives in a dream world where all the women love him...and why not let him dream? Poor Mongoloid, handed to us by mother nature so that in the middle of so much beauty we'd remember that bad things can happen to anyone. And what is bad anyway? Do we really know how much good can come from what's bad, and how much bad can come from what's good?"

Giacomino is always telling me about his orange groves, about the unavoidable difficulties of getting his babas to rise ("It doesn't look it, but they're the most difficult pastry—they have to leaven three times"), or about the local idiots and crazies ("Luckily there are not too many in our town. You should see Praiano!") with the same slow and calm tone, be it for a filling applied without a hitch or a child born with problems.

"Caruso was a great worker, then he started bouncing between Positano and America, and one night while he was over there he lost his memory, forgetting everything about his life and the world. He only remembers the tenor Caruso whom he listened to over there, though no one knows if at a theater or just on a record. Fact is, for twenty years he's been convinced he can hit the high C that was powerful enough to shatter the chandeliers in the Metropolitan...Ciccillo the Cemetery is called that because he only talks about deaths and other misfortunes."

"Actually, he only tells me about fantastic catches."

"Because you've seen him in the daytime...At night he gets going with his life story. Unfortunately, all of the things he says are true, but I've never understood if he invokes those memories because he's haunted by them, or if it's just the wine bringing them back to mind. But what're you going to do? You can't refuse him a glass... It's true that he was a great fisherman. Every day at sunrise he goes from his lodgings to the dock to find his boat. He gives it a shine, fiddles around in it, and probably imagines going fishing like he did back in the day. But as far as the sea is concerned, he hasn't gone out in twenty years. The nuns wanted to sell the boat since he hadn't paid board, but we didn't allow it. You want to take away that little toy, the last thing he has left after all of the children he lost to illness and war?"

I could never describe Giacomino's voice—a sinuous wisp of smoke mixed with the whiteness of his jasmine flowers and the aroma of orange blossoms at sunset? A sound never heard before, incorporeal but precise. Perhaps it's nothing more than the timbre that the angels must have had before the advent of the Christian era, in the time of Odysseus, and maybe even before...

The storm has stopped. Every afternoon it lets loose for two hours, and then everything ends in such pure peacefulness, intoxicating the senses more than any wine could. I feel like seeing Giacomino, and without worrying about *Metello*, my letters, or the woman's tea, I get dressed in a hurry and rush outside, where the sunset is lingering on the rocky walls, which are still glowing at the top in the day's final rays, and on the countless steps. Positano is the town of long sunsets. The sun, passing over the immense wall of hills, shines with an extreme brightness, spreading a premature shadow over the steps while the large expanse of sea is transformed into a burning glass that for hours and hours sets aflame the whites and pinks of the houses, the green of the lemon trees, the rusted red of the cliffs.

In Giacomino's small two-room café, too, the bright red of that movie-studio sunset dwells as if eternally held there by a mad director. I immediately spot my pre-Christian angel. His gentle face is white from the long nights of all bread and pastry artisans, while the flaming sunset colors his blue eyes amber. With a smile even more enigmatic than the timbre of his voice, he greets me as if he'd been expecting me. And at my "I need a coffee, Giacomino, I can't take these sunsets of yours anymore," he calmly whispers: "Your friend arrived and ordered two teas. She's in the other room . . . Or would you rather a coffee?"

"No, no. Tea, in that case."

Why am I not surprised to see her greet me when I enter the other room? Like that sunset or Giacomino's personality, she too is eternal—with her timeless gesturing, her melancholy as old as the world itself. Or her beauty, which every hour is renewed and changes its appearance: sometimes a slightly withered flower, sometimes a soft cloud, or—as it is now—a beautiful, colorful orange, pulsing with a joy for life. Her entire body is wrapped in a light, olive-green dress.

"The storm was too troublesome, and then the calm was too calm. So I thought I'd come see Giacomino. I left you a note by the entrance. You saw it, right?"

"No, to tell you the truth, I didn't notice it."

"Of course, you're new to the house. Anyone staying there can leave messages on the big table on the right."

"Good to know! And meanwhile, *I* had ditched you without giving it a second thought."

"Oh, but it's nicer this way!"

"It is hard to lose track of someone in this town."

"Actually, it's incredible, but if you want to, you can go without seeing anyone."

True, and I reflect on the most recent Positano mystery that has popped up in my head: "For two days now, I haven't seen either Pierpaolo or Lorenzo. Did they leave?"

"Oh no! It's just that in this maze of alleyways you're unlikely to run into someone by chance, unless you go down to the shore at certain times of day. And here it's common not to search too hard for anyone who has disappeared. Did you see Giacomino, the way he slipped away after bringing us the tea, even though he usually hangs around? It's the actual spirit of the place itself that suggested to him that we needed to be alone."

"To tell you the truth, I feel like Giacomino is dying to talk to us. Did you know that he was the one who encouraged me to meet you? Really—one afternoon I was sitting in here and we saw you pass by in a hurry through the window. The sun was shining so bright, you looked almost unreal. After I'd been following you with my eyes, he said, 'You should meet Erica, she's seen everything in this town.'"

"Giacomino has never made a single bad judgment concerning people or business." At the word "business" she lets out a high-pitched laugh, who knows why. Then she goes on speaking, her voice low and serious: "Listening to the spirit of this place and following its laws, you wouldn't believe how far I had to go to find a bit of free beach this morning. I was practically about to end up in Capri, a place my entire family detests. I actually don't mind Capri, but my parents were such snobs, even more so than me and Giacomino, if that's possible. On every beach today there was a towel, a pair of shoes, or a rubber raft. As hard as I tried not to look, they were all taken by couples—the usual local guy resting his head on a Valkyrie's shoulder or huge breasts. Our dark boys sure like to climb those soft mountains of white, whipped-cream flesh and sink their hungry lips into those masses of cotton-candy hair... If the women are actually ugly in their features, they don't notice, they're so blinded by the pinkish and golden shimmering of blond body hair... Oh, did you hear the news? They settled the dispute over the mayor's English wife—a real medieval duel, even if it was disguised with judges' and lawyers' robes."

"What dispute?" I need to ask, unfortunately interrupting the enchanting wave that is her voice when she's telling a story.

"You don't know? I'll start from the beginning then. Two years ago, the English ambassador came here on an unofficial visit with his extremely refined wife—more than a woman, I'd say a mystical breath of air from her toes to her demure, golden chignon, a nature lover, completely devoted to studying plants, and, as a hobby of course, to garden planning. Well, by the end of her third day she goes to her husband and declares: 'I'm not going back to England, I've fallen in love with the mayor of this town, plus there are acres upon acres of Mediterranean flora to study here. This is the place for me. God gave it to me and not you nor the queen herself can take it away from me.' The ambassador replies coolly: 'Fine, darling, you can do what you wish, but you'll never see your daughters again.' 'We'll see about that,' she says. 'Goodbye then, darling.' Just in the last few days, after the divorce, the beautiful garden queen, as they now call her throughout the entire Coast, married the mayor, and is not only expecting his child, but she also gained custody of her two daughters, who are due to arrive any day now. You can't imagine how happy the town is! They've followed the story over the last few years—from opposing factions, of course—with only slightly less intensity than they did the fondly remembered Coppi-Bartali rivalry.* Personally, I quite like this series of events with its triumphant ending. I don't know about you, but I'm so sick of tragic stories."

"Well, I was already tired of them when I was sixteen. Should we go home or do you want to look for Pierpaolo?"

"I ran into him while I was walking down here, he was playing his flute and asked if he could see you. It seems trite to say, but he's so sweet and sylvan with his sublime voice and boyish grace...I can't imagine what a hard

---

* Fausto Coppi and Gino Bartali were two cycling champions whose rivalry captivated Italy, likely more than any other phenomenon in sports, throughout the 1940s and early 1950s.

time he must have had in that awful family he grew up in! Thank goodness his inner soundness brought him here, and if he doesn't let himself become sidetracked by the sirens of making money and having a career, he'll still be a boy when he's ninety years old. He's not the first one to stay that way in a place like this. I mean, can you figure out how old Giacomino is, or his wife? People never grow old here, like in Shangri-La. The secret is in never getting too far from these stairs. Countless times I've been tempted to sell everything and hole up here. Unfortunately, there's also part of me that loves the big cities, the gloomy traffic of London and New York. And then there's my passion for paintings and all of those magnificent beasts who make them and who now count on me like a new Peggy Guggenheim. I'm not ashamed to admit that I'd like to become like her over time, even if it'll mean risking my entire fortune, and my life, which is always in danger whenever I leave my enchanted Shangri-La."

While listening to her voice, I forget my hunger and don't notice the long and tiring late-evening walk uphill, nor do I realize it when we enter the house and sit down to eat in front of a lentil-and-escarole soup that's just like the one Lucibello's wife makes. Only the smell of that soup brings me back to reality. Or was it the sudden silence that, as always, is emanating from the white of the tablecloth, or from the crystal, or from the centerpiece of flowers and fruit murmuring an ancient prayer and kindling in us a reverence for wine, for bread?

For how long now have I been eating, sleeping, living in this house? Forever, I think, maybe even since before I was born. And I know I shouldn't—in my house too we were prohibited from breaking that silence—but my sudden panic over the fact that I'll soon have to leave makes me shout out: "I don't want to die! No, no—I wanted to say that I don't want to go, to go away from here!"

"There's no reason for you to die, and more importantly, you can stay here as long as you like. Even if I need to leave, you can stay. Or are you worried about your man? Have him come if you like, there's room. You could both work here, even."

Those words—I've heard them before, when? In another life? Who knows what evokes the sensation of déjà-vu that assails us out of nowhere as we run about our day-to-day lives? But the words seep into me, like a lullaby, and I make up my mind to look at her. She has set down her utensils to speak, and she is waiting for me to respond.

"Oh, thank you, Erica. I'm glad, and I think I'll take you up on your offer, thank you."

After the coffee, friends of Erica's, both Italians and foreigners, began to arrive in droves, and life resumed some semblance of reality, though still highly drugged as it was by the profound darkness of the sea and the sky, which from the wide-open windows made the lounge feel like a small ghost ship, floating in a metaphysical atmosphere.

· 11 ·

During my first stay in that house perched at the edge of reality, with its terraces and balconies flung out as far as possible into the emptiness—a dizzying taste of the small step that separates being from nonbeing—I developed a habit (a misguided one, or extremely clarifying?) of periodically stepping outside of myself by getting lost in the stones, the colors, the sand, the cliffs, the sun, though always in the protective shadow of the house's walls, as sturdy as the solid structure that constituted its owner's personality.

On more than one occasion in those years I was able to witness firsthand her physical and moral strength. The first time was when a full-fledged hurricane surprised us just off Capo Palinuro, and she calmly escaped it, steering the boat farther out before zigzagging intricately by the rock crags and sheer cliff walls toward the shore with a mathematical precision I found incomprehensible. Frozen stiff and exhausted from the furious winds and waves, we brought the small skiff back into harbor, thanks, too, to the sudden calm—even more frightening for its precariousness—that was lapping against the rocky beach of Positano.

And there was the time when I had lain down drunk on a marble bench in Piazzetta dei Mulini and, with total drunken stubbornness, had wanted to stay there to die. I was only happy, and *dying* just stood for *sleeping*; I remember that she picked me up and carried me all the way up to the house.

"How in the world did you manage?" I ask next to her in the winter sitting room by the large fireplace which lights her with faint flickers, making her appear so thin and diaphanous in her white pants and wooly sweater as soft as kitten's fur.

"Oh, Pierpaolo helped me!"

For some time, we had started seeing each other in Positano during the winter as well. In that time of year, a crystal light would make the town possibly even more metaphysical than it was in the summer, allowing the eye to decipher at a distance even the smallest details of the rocks, the trees, and the houses. Maybe it was a bad idea to meet also in that season of regrets and confessions, of "slumber," and of nostalgia for the past. Maybe. But who can say what is good or bad in a life, in a relationship, or in lost love? In the end, it was further understanding, and this word—as we all know—always brings with it pain.

"Did you know, Goliarda, the American girl from Dallas, Marilyn, Alfonso the Shark's girlfriend—she's coming back this spring? Alfonso is happy. She put together the sum that he'd set in order to marry her—who knows how she earned it—and yesterday he came to ask me for that cubbyhole I have just off Piazzetta dei Mulini. I sold it to him, I almost wanted to give it to him for free, seeing how happy he was. But better to leave him the incentive to earn things for himself. I gave it to him at a more than reasonable price. He wants to open a little waterskiing school. That way, while she takes care of renting out rooms, she can also spread the word about the school, since she speaks English. Alfonso is planning on starting this year. She's the one who taught him the sport: ten years ago, she came here with her nice skis, she was really just a kid then, and she was so distraught when she found out we still didn't have motorboats here! So now they'll have their little business. The whole town is waiting for the Shark's fiancée, just as they waited for—remember?—Helen's daughters to get here, the woman who's now the mayor's wife. All the bets that have been made over the last year . . . Will Marilyn find the money? Will she fall in love with someone else? And May is still so many months away. Some are still betting that she won't come. How can such a well-educated girl, raised in the golden America we all dream of, shut herself away in this backwater town? But knowing the town as I do, I'm sure she'll come! It will be a happy ending for once.

I think it's wonderful! I've only known unhappy love... Is being rich such a great sin it should deny you the possibility of having untroubled love? And yet my mother and father must have savored their love for one another to the fullest, seeing as after he died she locked herself away in such an eerily untroubled silence that nature was forced to free her from life on the very same day of his death, only a year later. Their love was 'scandalous' for us children, we were unconsciously jealous of it. Sure, they had their fights, but it always ended with the offering of some bottle of champagne or fine wine from my father's cellar. He loved only the natural sciences and wine. He hated people and, in particular, the female sex."

"What was your childhood home like?"

"Oh, ask that question to any writer who's written the story of a wealthy family without being born into it—into wealth, I mean. Maybe only they can truly see it, looking in from the outside. Or maybe they just re-create those homes from their decor books and museums, or, worse still, from the immortal *War and Peace* or *Anna Karenina*. Even with Thomas Mann you get the feeling he's describing a kind of wealth that's already foreign to him...Proust, did you say? I've never read him, I've always been afraid to. I see I've left you speechless. I don't mean to diminish these authors' genius. In fact, for me their description of wealth is enchanting, moving. It's realer than reality itself...Ours was so completely natural and monotonous, just another part of my day-to-day life—to the point that when I lost it for a brief period, it was like the rug had been pulled out

from under me, the way someone might feel if they lost
bread and butter . . .

But going back to the places of my childhood, I only
remember large spaces, bright and fragrant interiors, and
fields, trees, flowers. Naturally, there were many horses,
and lots of tennis, which had already been brought over
much earlier by the English, who were the first foreigners
to settle down in the Tuscan countryside. When my two
sisters and I would go in the spring to see my father's sisters in Syracuse, tennis was not even spoken of. They ab-
horred it for the exposed legs of the women and, as Aunt
Myrta would always say, for that spasmodic way of running
around, so crude for anyone who would call herself a lady.

Our Sicilian aunts said that my dad was born with a
nomadic instinct and that it would bring us to ruin. They
were right, because keeping four houses open all the time
in Florence, Milan, Rome, and Sorrento was like a gambling addiction, at least in terms of how much it cost to live
that way—insane according to our aunts, and wonderful to
us. I'm somewhat ashamed to admit it, now that people are
so into unhappy childhoods, but mine was so wonderful,
a real fairy tale, I'm afraid no poet will ever take it into
consideration . . .

Dad bought this house in 1932, the Amalfi Coast was a
late discovery of his. Money was already starting to dry up
a bit, so he settled for what he called 'the pied-à-terre.' The
only minor sadness our parents caused for us was due to
how strikingly close they were. We felt somewhat excluded,
but we saw them so infrequently—at lunch and sometimes

at dinner. And besides, once we were out of that dining room, each of us girls could choose her own person to love from the many possibilities our family clan had to offer: there were other boys and girls—our cousins—along with our very young uncles and aunts. Which is to say that anyone looking to experience an exclusive and profound kind of love wasn't lacking in options. I picked a cousin who was four years older than me. I can still picture him perfectly, but I can't describe him, just as you can't describe the face of love: seeing him was to become excited about an otherwise ordinary day, to rejoice over a rainy afternoon simply because he was there reading poetry, or was next to you playing a piano you previously hated for its scales and solfège and Clementi sonatinas. I never had much of a knack for music. If he hadn't been the one, with his loving fingertips, touching those keys...

When I was eleven, I had already decided I'd marry him. My mother had also met my father at that age. I didn't tell anyone besides Olivia, my younger sister, who represented that other love, the sisterly kind—tribal, you could say. I led her deep into the forest, despite the biting cold that terrible winter, and made her swear she'd keep the secret, or else she and I would be cursed to lose the love holding us together. I can't imagine what kind of effort the poor girl had to make to always keep that secret! It's too bad that life shatters our impulse toward the lofty and heroic.

Riccardo—that was my love's name—also kept our bond a secret, and this understanding between the three of us made it so thrilling every time we'd sneak into the

greenhouse, the attic, or the woods, where quickly exchanging a hidden kiss or caress seemed like the kind of
slightly sinful act of disobedience that has strengthened
and prolonged love since the world began. And then there
were long periods of time when Riccardo would be away
studying in England, or the awful summers when his
mother would force her only son to go on a *Bildungsreise*,
to Germany—she was half German—or to Greece. Once he
was sent to the Netherlands. I remember when he came
back, more enthusiastic than ever, saying: 'It seems absurd
for an Italian to discover the art of painting in Holland,
but to me their old masters are one hundred times greater
and less affected than ours. Go ahead, laugh, but I'll be a
painter, and a Dutch one. Come on, let's go buy canvases
and brushes.' And when I asked him, 'Why didn't you buy
all of that in your precious Holland?' he replied: 'I might
be an artist, but I'm not naive! They cost less here in Florence, my dear.' They were such magnificent afternoons,
trailing behind that boy, who already knew loads about
canvases and colors, through all of the shops in Florence;
also because, in addition to the secret of our love, we now
had this second secret, his budding talent as a painter. To
make everything more enthralling, he made me swear—as
I had done with Olivia—not to say a thing about it to anyone. If I did, it would be the end of our now time-honored
understanding."

12

"*Riccardo was very precise* with money, which, I'd realize later, was something he had picked up from his English grandmother. He was pragmatic in a way that was so exotic to Italians like us, it sometimes made him seem cold and a bit cynical in my parents' eyes. My father would grumble, 'That boy is too disenchanted for his age.' On top of that, he had this soldierly attitude, even in a sports jacket, as if underneath his shirt he wore some kind of armored breastplate. In his clear, gray eyes, when this warrior side would show itself, there would flash visions of battles and duels, with victory practically in sight. To give you an idea, when we weren't even children anymore, he'd have us play squire and lady of the castle, telling me of all of the jousts and

tournaments he'd had to fight in order to win me over and
bear my colors, which he said were gold and white. His ancestors on his father's side had all been men of arms in the
past, and, at present, he had an admiral grandfather, and
a father who'd had to settle for becoming a cavalry officer
since he had the bad luck of suffering from seasickness. I
really liked his father, the colonel, that big, good-natured
man with his full head of blond hair. He would caress my
head so tenderly I couldn't help but love him. Those physical signs of affection, like kisses or hugs, weren't allowed
in my house, except on special occasions like New Year's,
or when you came back from a faraway country or a relative
had died. Unfortunately, that oversized good-naturedness
was, as far as my father was concerned, the cause of the
tight circumstances into which he had been dragging Riccardo's family for the last twenty years: 'He got fat at the
gambling tables, the fool! Where's the fun in losing money
and gaining weight so inelegantly? Tell me, where's the joy
in that? If he needs to ruin himself physically, he could at
least do it with others at the dinner table, enjoying some
food and our top-notch wine.'

When my father spoke this way about the man whom
I secretly hoped would become my second father, I don't
know why, but I'd start to cry. Sadly, I'd understand later.
Those childish tears were an unconscious foreshadowing
of the Cassandra inside of me. Every woman has in her—
along with a Circe, Juno, Judith, and Athena—a Cassandra,
who sometimes makes her weep and shake with yearning,
in a way that she herself doesn't understand and men find

foolish. But I see that I've bored you a bit with my love story. Love is so sappy and meandering.

Going back to the tiny Cassandra hidden in my little girl's body, who had made me tremble so many times when faced with my parents' hostility—even if inexplicit— toward my love's family: she was right. In agony, that day—I was only sixteen—I made up my mind to declare to my father that Riccardo and I wanted to get married. I listened to his reply, which wasn't the least bit irate or disdainful: 'Well, I warned your mother, I said that too much time with the cousins would lead to drama. Don't even think about it. He doesn't have a cent. I could even accept it at the end of the day, but you'll see that he'll be the one not to want to go through with it. He's growing up properly, our Riccardo, a true man of honor, and he knows that he can't ruin your life by pulling you into destitution.' 'But we have money!' 'I said that he's a man of honor, and honor forces a man not to depend on others. Let's not talk about it anymore.'

As you can imagine, I fell into a state of pure distress. I went to Riccardo, and without batting an eyelash he confirmed word for word what my father had said. After a pause, he added: 'I know it was a beautiful dream. All children hope that a miracle might someday come to the rescue, but it's not the way things work... Don't cry, though!'

I didn't understand the reason for that 'Don't cry.' I didn't feel a single tear on my face. He, on the other hand, suddenly looked as pale as a dead man, and I needed to shut my eyes and not look at that corpse which was talking to me just as in a nightmare. He said that with time, if he made his own fortune or I became poor, we could find each other again. But since these hopeful words had made me reopen my eyes, Riccardo turned his face up, almost to avoid my presence, and yelled: 'For goodness' sake, Erica, let's not keep adding one mistake on top of the other! It's an impossible dream ... but it was beautiful, and will be a beautiful memory that will help us throughout our lives. Think of the two of us: poor, together ... It would only end up destroying our precious past.'

After this conversation, I only remember that someone told me he had left for North America, maybe to go teach at some shabby college. Then I fell ill. Anemia, they said. I only knew that life had lost all its flavor. I won't say that I wanted to die, but I no longer found anything pleasing in foods, smells, colors. And on top of anemia, they added the word 'tuberculosis,' and they started to move me around like an object, or rather like an inanimate doll, constantly looked after and perfumed, all around the Swiss mountains. It was there, with brief intervals in the Taormina winter sun, that I became a passionate reader.

Only by sinking into those extraordinary structures that are the great novels could I find any escape from the pain of living, which was slowly turning into a kind of detachment from everything, a sadness that was even sweet at times, the way writers probably feel when they bring their heroine's story onto the page. Emotionless, I saw myself from the outside, to the extent that like a 'creator,' I began to choose my way of walking, speaking, dressing. The attention I gave to myself, to every one of my thoughts, gestures, and looks, turned me into what I am—'perfect,' as my friend Morgan says, but he's an aesthete...I'm also affected and guarded, I realize that, and who knows what else I could have become. Maybe a precious Pre-Raphaelite statue. Like my older sister, Fiore, always used to say: 'One of these days we'll have no choice but to put you in the empty niche in the living room in place of the statue Dad had removed, seeing as you're so dead set on turning to stone—although the precious kind, of course.' Surely I would have ended up in that niche, hidden from the light of day, if it hadn't been for my father's death. It was unexpected, a sudden failing of the heart, as they called heart attacks back then, the very thing he had so often said he hoped for as an elegant exit from life's stage. He died in his quiet study, his beautiful head with its thick curly blond hair resting against the back of his armchair, a book on botany open in his lap, and a magnifying glass in his hand. Only the tight grip of those tapered, almost feminine fingers indicated the brief agony he had felt in passing.

He went the same way he had lived, without any fuss. But you can only imagine the dismay when we opened his will. The only thing he'd left us was a trail of debts. The news was a blow to all of us, including the servants, who, poor things, had hoped to inherit something. It turned our world upside down, like a hail storm in the middle of June, and swept away all of the shining and golden promises for the future...The house shook from its very foundations, and the souls within it, disregarding all rules of refinement, trembled and cried out in despair. And in their cries was a touch of hatred for the deceased, even from my mother, Fiore, the butler (who started to get drunk, dipping into our wine cellar), and the governess, who for twenty years had been perfect in her dedication to us.

For me, that sudden earthquake only helped wake me from my prolonged sleep, giving me a vital shock for our future. My fear, though, was mixed with a huge amount of curiosity, as if something living had finally stirred inside the tomb in which I had buried myself. And it was a good thing it happened, too, because it allowed me to take affairs into my own hands, and avoid the worst disasters that the lawyers and public officials were getting ready to throw at us, like rats scurrying off a sinking ship. As often happens in these cases, all of our relatives disappeared, and nearly all our friends with them. Only one of them, Licata, a childhood friend of my father's who worked in the Court of Audit, stayed by my side, and with him I was at least able to scrape together enough money to compensate our oldest servants and guarantee my mother another year or two of relative comfort in that house. She was deaf to all reasoning and refused to leave. The worst part was that she'd say so with this wry smile stamped on her beautiful lips: 'I was born here, I lived here just like my mother, my grandmother, and great-grandmother, and here I'll die. You can all go. I have to stay.'

And there she stayed, even without servants, in that empty house with no furniture, tapestries, or paintings—everything had been auctioned off! She shut herself away in her rooms and stopped speaking, even with her eyes.

Going by what our nanny told me, she lived only on tea and cookies. I essentially never saw her again—I was so busy—while she slowly let herself die. Perhaps I had seen her so often in the past that I could feel that she was slipping away.

Exactly a year after my father's death, she followed him into that other world, peaceful and untroubled. She could no longer live without him, the nanny told us as she packed her bags to return to her little village in the north, near Trento, where thankfully the dear old woman still had sisters who were willing to take her in. In any case, at least she could go there with some money we had managed to scrounge together for her. Now a seal was placed even on those last rooms, the ones that had been kept open until my mother's death. And with a feeling of relief—we didn't know what kind of vulgar existence we were heading toward—we three sisters took a few suitcases and a trunk, and we moved to Milan. Licata had found us a small apartment there, and, through his friends, some German lessons for Fiore and another position for me. What could we have done in Florence, where no one wanted to offer us some lousy job, since they all still felt too much respect or were too intimidated by our former wealth—that's what our protector told us. But seeing how, at the auction, they threw themselves like jackals onto our furniture and paintings and furs, what Licata called their respect or esteem seemed to me to be their way of mocking us.

That's how Prince Beneventano's three treasures, feeling more shock than sorrow, took three first-class train tickets—payed for, as always, by our benefactor—to Milan, a city that, while not far, was unfamiliar to us. We had already toured the city of Stendhal once after an evening at La Scala, but none of us could pretend she knew the streets and squares of the city's daily life. I won't go into the details of how we settled into our 'little pad,' where a fat woman stinking of soup and fried food led us in, saying: 'It was my aunt's most beautiful apartment, and I wouldn't have given it to anyone low-class. Wait till you see how much light it gets in the spring.' This jewel of an apartment was at the top of an absurd, twentieth-century construction, like a pyramid of stacked cardboard boxes. It had no balconies, no elevator, and faced a giant boulevard swarming like a beehive with furious and depressing traffic. The three of us sat around a ridiculously large table for that small space pompously referred to as a dining room, staring at one another, still bundled up in our coats, our shut suitcases cluttering the whole entrance with its nice Tyrolese coatrack, waiting for the woman to make up her mind to leave us alone.

When she finally left, slamming the door loudly behind her, we all broke out into laughter. It was so spontaneous that it seemed like a good omen to me, and I clung to it with all my might, trying to forget the pallor that had already spread over Fiore's cheeks in the train, and the barely held-back tears in young Olivia's eyes at the sight of the immense terminus of dirty iron and glass in the Milan train station. But that laughter—like a joyful echo of a shared piece of our childhoods—was the first and last to ring out in those three cramped rooms, where for the first time in our lives we needed to make a schedule for taking turns in the bathroom. We never could have imagined that washing up was a privilege reserved for the few. But I don't want to bore you with all this gloom. Fiore, once again thanks to our protector, quickly started to give Latin and German lessons—you know how much German was in vogue then, they said it was going to be the language of the future—but she was paid below average since she didn't have a diploma and had to compete with so many starving professors who had all the necessary bells and whistles. Luckily, despite our ridiculous education, Fiore had actually studied languages, thanks to her own talent and to a scrupulousness inherited from our father."

13

"*I was dying to* start that job Licata had promised me. But Olivia? What could she do after sixteen years ignorantly spent at the piano, at the harp, or singing songs? She had to bear the whole burden of the house. In the first few months, I at least tried to help her get the hang of normal expenses like groceries. You might find it hard to believe, but she was afraid of going into the neighborhood shops, where loud, curt men overwhelmed her with jokey compliments. They thought it would help buck her up, but she only became more frightened. Olivia, unlike me and Fiore, was and is a truly striking beauty. She looked like Ava Gardner, to give you an idea. You'll be amazed when you meet her, because she almost seems older than me. While I helped her to go out and face the streets, shops, and markets, an absurd idea began to work its way into my thoughts: that our father, instead of being an enlightened Westerner as he liked to define himself, was nothing but a sultan or an ancient Chinese patriarch, and that unwittingly—with that magnificent geisha, our mother, as an accomplice—he had mutilated our little feet, and consequently our minds. That's how difficult it was for us to stay standing, still wearing shoes that were too soft and thin for those hard and muddy paved streets...So, when I got my first paycheck, I bought myself a nice pair of wide-soled, low-heeled boots, and even though Olivia screamed that they were the ugliest things she'd ever seen, I felt much better when I'd run in the early morning to catch the crowded tram as it roared along like a pirate ship.

You won't believe it, but the day I received that first paycheck was the day I was truly born, to life and to joy. If only it could have gone on that way. I'm sure that from that first little job as a salesgirl at the Rinascente department store I could have gone a long way, even in an insignificant world like that one. Since I was pleasant enough to look at and knew how to pronounce the names of French perfumes, they put me in the cosmetics department.

Although it was hard getting up early every morning, it was a relief to escape that house and to spend the whole day away from it. At home, even if I tried not to see it, things were not going well at all. Fiore was losing weight at a scary rate, and Olivia, our joyous, singing Olivia, once always ready to crack a joke, now hardly spoke—and when she did, she always had a sharp tone for Fiore and me. Was it the lack of physical space? Or was it the broom she was always clutching, the overflowing sink, the heavy packages she had to carry up five flights every day? With me, especially, that bad mood of hers would come out so often that my heart would ache whenever I'd have to come back home in the evening. I had only a lunch break during the day, which I'd spend with the other Rinascente saleswomen—amazing girls—lively, strong, and many of them, I'd learn later, were anti-Fascists too.

But why was Olivia upset with me especially? Because, from the day we'd stepped foot in that apartment, she had started arguing that I should look for Riccardo. Hadn't he said that if I ever wound up poor he could marry me then? I disagreed, saying that besides the distance separating us with him still in America, Riccardo wouldn't have been able to help me with the small professor's salary he made over there. But she didn't believe it. She was convinced—partly due to the way we were raised—that a man can do anything, and that, therefore, he could have saved us. She insisted so much, I eventually tried to find out more just to keep her calm, and I learned that he had gotten married to an American colleague.

The news—I sure had been right not to look for him before!—cracked my broken heart back open, after it had barely healed the first time. It was nothing excruciating though, I only felt a light, melancholic nostalgia for that old dream of love. I probably never was very sentimental. I hoped in vain to quiet down Olivia with that piece of information, but the result left me stunned: my sister lost it, crying desperately and yelling, 'So nothing is real, it's all a lie! It's better to die then!'

Her emotional crisis lasted a full month. Fiore looked after her with the patience of a saint, until Olivia eventually started to act like herself again. But one morning, surprised not to see Fiore up and around the house yet, I opened the door to her room... My sister was lying in her bed, which was soaked with blood. She had cut open her veins in both wrists, and she was already dead. On the bedside table, under the lamp still sinisterly lit, there was a letter: 'To Olivia and Erica, my dear sisters.' The piece of paper inside also began 'Olivia and Erica.' Then: 'My dear sisters, forgive me, I love you deeply, but Olivia is right, there's no truth or love in this world, only lies. I'm sorry, I love you but I can't go on anymore...' This new tragedy acted like a clarifying filter within me, revealing how completely misguided our lives had been under the protective wings of privilege. I also saw how absurd the abstract path mapped out by bogus literature can be—think of *Like Falling Leaves* by Giacosa.* Do you know it? The whole edifying struggle of Nennéle, the heroic little sister who saves the family from financial ruin!

No dedication to honest work could have saved me; or maybe it could have saved *me*, having oddly enough been

---

* *Come le foglie* is a 1900 comedy–drama by Giuseppe Giacosa. Though Giacosa was most active as a playwright, he is principally remembered today for his work as a librettist, having written the librettos for Giacomo Puccini's operas *La bohème*, *Tosca*, and *Madama Butterfly*.

different from my mother and my sisters since the day I was born—a difference that I tried afterward to analyze without any major discovery—but not Olivia.

In that northern morning, just barely lit by the glow coming from the small bedside lamp, I thought that she wouldn't make it either. Seeing all that blood, and Fiore's beautiful face, so peaceful in death even if horribly gaunt, like the sweet face of a wax saint, all of it was inviting Olivia to follow her on the only path left to escape the squalor into which life had tossed us. Hadn't my mother always said that it was better to die than to stoop to vulgarity, to meanness, to pure self-interest?

My mother's words echoed in Fiore's face, and Olivia, sitting motionless next to me without a tear in her eyes, agreed completely. In only a few seconds, as apparently happens when you drown or are led to the electric chair, every key moment of my young life flashed before my eyes with frightening detail. In these scenes, I saw the bond between Olivia and Fiore, a bond I had not wanted to see before, because I was jealous or too superficial. Sure, Olivia spent more time with me than with Fiore, but now I knew it was just because she had fun with me. I was her holiday, while only with her other sister did she find a true mirror to her feelings, and thereby real nourishment.

Until that catastrophe, Olivia, with youth's healthy and knowing sense of balance, would come to me to 'learn' to live joyously and—why not?—frivolously, but only after absorbing depth, a sense of morality, and culture from Fiore, who, without a doubt, was the one who 'stood the tallest' of the three Beneventano girls.

Even for me, before Olivia was born, hadn't Fiore been my example of grace, of discretion, of depth? And the logical conclusion of that lucid journey back through our past was that if I could have rivaled Fiore's influence over Olivia while she was alive, now that she was dead she assumed an unbeatable power in my little sister's mind. This power revealed itself immediately—if you knew to look for it—in her decision to take care of the deceased all by herself, and she practically shooed me away when I moved to help her. Another sign, possibly even more alarming than the others, was how she actually preferred our landlady's help, since someone had to give her a hand in removing Fiore's mortal remains, washing them, and then remaking the bed.

There was nothing I could do for the time being. Even if I managed to keep going because of my incredibly cold mentality (a coldness that later would astound even me), I was also stung with such a painful feeling of grief for Fiore's death, I could never even describe it: like losing a limb or an eye. And it might seem thankless to my parents, but to this day hers is the sole passing that stays stuck in my mind—her absence alone feels like an unfillable void. Olivia's words were kind yet final as she sent me away from that little room now consecrated by Fiore's death, telling me I had to go to work: 'You care so much about that job, and I'd hate to see you lose it . . .'

I was shaking, I felt nearly dizzy, as after a solemn bout of drinking. I went into my room to get dressed, I grabbed my practical boots, and after staring at them for a while, I threw them into a corner. Then, without knowing what I was doing—is it possible to start sleepwalking while awake?—at a certain point I found myself inside a taxi in an elegant dress, my feet feeling light and a bit cold in my old suede shoes, touching up my face in a compact mirror...And then I was sitting on a couch in the large living room belonging to my father's only brother, Alessandro. His chubby, somewhat foolish-looking face seemed deeply moved for once. What had I told him?

After a moment of silence, and turning away to conceal a tear, he took my hand in his, which was fat and soft like a nun's, and said: 'You poor girls! But don't be afraid, I'll be the one to take care of everything now. Oh, if I'd only been in Italy at the time! But my work, this damn work which is always taking me farther and farther away...Now I have some things to do, but come here tomorrow morning, and then, as you rightly suggested, we'll lay out a plan to save Olivia and yourself as well, even if I can see your strength, your courage. Yes, forgive me, but we also have to think about you, whom I've always admired so much.'

I had gone to my father's only brother, and his only enemy. He'd hated him since they were children—you know, that familial rivalry that has always reappeared since the time of Cain, and which perhaps only between brothers can become so irreparably intense, like something out of Dante. My sisters and I had never even gotten a glimpse of the man, had only heard about him from our nanny, but it was always a great secret, one we had to promise we wouldn't repeat to my father and mother. They almost never mentioned him; when it did happen, it was only for questions of inheritance or by accident, though they'd always refer to him the way one does to the devil, or, in the south, to someone who's just as bad or who brings bad luck: 'that one!' In stories too, 'that one' was the opposite of my father. Intelligent, but malicious, greedy, and cynical, only interested in his career and in making money; and, due to this greed, he never had any qualms about always siding with the victor, even in politics. He had made his fortune in America. He'd been a liberal supporter of Giolitti, but he immediately became a die-hard Fascist once Mussolini came to power, and, most recently, such a fervent Nazi that even Germans themselves had to admire him.

But the thing that had really annoyed my father was that his brother had always stolen his young sweethearts, and even, when they'd grown up, a wonderful girl who had been his great love before he met my mother. He had stolen her without giving it a second thought, only to dump her because she was poor. Even up to that point, going by what our nanny said, my uncle still would see the family on occasion, but when he tried to attract the attention of the woman who would go on to be our mother, my father threw him out of the house, trying, it seems, to rough him up in the process, too. The problem was that Alessandro was also physically strong, and my father took such a walloping he really did risk losing my mother, because if there's one thing a woman just can't bear it's seeing her man re-duced to a bloody pulp by a rival, as our nanny commented. 'Oh, I felt so awful for my two little doves!'—those were her words. 'You could really see how upset the girl was, and she was blurting out alarming things like *My God, why attack someone—even if you're in the right—when you know they're stronger, why? Why did you do it? It's awful!'* We laughed at these stories, to the great dismay of our nanny, who would shoo us away from the big kitchen with her broom."

· 14 ·

"*How could I* have gone to him, I thought, torturing myself as I came back home. And how in the world did I remember his exact address, which Licata had given me once. Licata looked embarrassed as he told me, 'I know that it would be unthinkable for you, but maybe in some extreme circumstances... Plus, Alessandro was the only one of your relatives who wrote to me before to offer to help you all. I referred the message to your mother, but she just scolded me: *Don't you see? That one has only popped up now to steal his brother's daughters. Don't you see that to him, it would represent the ultimate victory over his hated brother?'*

Licata's words were torturing me so much, I think it took me an hour to go up the five flights to our apartment: I had to keep stopping to sit, my legs had gone soft and weak. 'I've betrayed my father's memory,' my knees rattled at me as they trembled like an old woman's, 'and no good can come from that.' But as soon as I walked into the apartment, Olivia's face, which in two hours had taken on the exact same pallor of the dead girl, like ancient ivory, now revealed indisputably the similarity between her and her sister. For a moment, I had a panic attack, pure and simple. Fiore, continuing to act with the passionate possessiveness that had always characterized her personality, had left her now cold body and seeped into that other, living self. This second Fiore was standing right in front of me with the same intensity and severity in her eyes as the original. That's what woke me up completely, calling me back to reality, and consequently into action. Which turned out to be incredibly easy, because that uncle of mine joyfully and enthusiastically welcomed all of the moral and practical obstacles I threw at him like a little boy discovering a beautiful Meccano toy underneath the Christmas tree. While he gracefully tore apart all of my objections one by one, I realized that this 'monster,' apart from the slight feminine flabbiness that enveloped his body—and maybe his soul too?—had the most beautiful and dreamy eyes I had ever seen in a man; they were like a teenager's, though he must have been a good deal over fifty. How could he be the brother of my father, who was so sad, so distant from everything that wasn't his collection of butterflies, his books, his mother and his wife (the only human beings who knew how to instill in him some feeling of love or respectful submissiveness, and not even all the time)?

I was sitting there in front of him, completely lost in all of these memories, when my uncle declared with a shrill hurrah: 'I've figured out how to avoid making Olivia suspicious when you two suddenly become wealthy again. I'll call Borletti now, he's a compassionate man and he'll understand. I'll ask him to move you along in your career, but it'll just be pretend, of course: I'll be the one paying your salary. We'll be accomplices, the two of us—you have no idea how much I like the idea! Believe it or not, Olivia's sullenness is a source of delight for me—it's part of our family heritage, she's just like my mother was, that moralist bore. I've always liked secrets, bluffs. Did you know I was once a great poker player? And as a child I dreamed of becoming a spy...That's it, it'll be like working as a spy, and with a magnificent companion to boot. How wonderful, we'll see each other in secret without her knowing, like two lovers. It's a shame I'm not married! We would've had two obstacles to get around and four eyes to hide from, doubling the thrill of secrecy...But you go straight home now with the news that you've been promoted. I'll make sure that tomorrow, at the Rinascente, you'll find a contract waiting for you, one I'll work out with my friend Borletti. Then, with this contract in hand, you can pretend to go looking for a better place to live. I have an apartment behind the Duomo, it's small but lovely. Here's the address, and also one for the store where you can go after to choose any furniture you'd like. But remember, you have to learn everything by heart like a real spy, I wouldn't want your sister to . . . My executive will put together a contract, it'll be the real deal, though with a merely symbolic sum, of course. And I think that'll do for today. Go on, kiddo, goodbye. How beautiful you are! I'm almost sorry that . . . yes, that I'm your uncle, and old.'

I didn't tell you about Fiore's funeral, and I won't now, it was too awful . . . I was so distracted by Alessandro's personality, by the hatching of our little 'affair,' as he called it, that I almost didn't notice Olivia anymore, nor did I remember how I'd felt before seeing him. In truth, it was almost painful for me to discover how much I too enjoyed myself as I followed his instructions and noticed how well he knew the women of our family and the outside world. To give you an example, the next morning I was terribly embarrassed about showing up in that place where for a year I'd only played the role of a little model salesgirl, and I was afraid of the reactions of the other girls in the department. But when, even from the entrance, I saw people's respect as they practically bowed to greet me, a feeling of disdain immediately followed by amusement forced me to acknowledge that, at least as far as our life on earth is concerned, Alessandro was right: everything is a bluff, a game, and all one can do is either accept its rules or perish.

When I saw Olivia's silent yet undeniable joy as soon as she stepped foot into that new apartment, crying one last time, I thought, for that painful past—calling out to Fiore amid her sobs, 'Oh, why didn't you wait just a few months?

Why didn't you have faith in life?'—I finally understood that even morality for morality's sake can be a deadly weapon, for ourselves and for others. Then I cried too, finally in my sister's arms again. But they were tears of regret—yes, regret for not having turned to that devil immediately, because I could have saved my Fiore too, kept her untouched and beautiful in her one-of-a-kind seriousness and sweetness. I also understood that in all family units—just as in nations—there's always someone who needs to come to grips with the world's demons in order to assure others the luxury of their moral utopia. Probably our house had fallen into ruin because my father had refused that role, but I had decided to assume it fully by that point. Even if my happiness was perhaps due more to some hidden delinquent side of mine than to a desire to do good—I was basically having the time of my life following *that one*'s plans—when I heard Olivia's tears of relief, I decided, still in each other's arms, to put to bed all of the moralizing that had been our family's bread and butter, and to strike out on my own path. In part because, following my second meeting with Alessandro, I immediately ran up against a feeling so strange and unthinkable it made me toss aside all of the old myths about his wickedness and my own morality. You want to know what it was? I wanted to see him, to hear once more his childish laugh, his schemes, his fantastical stories about his own wrongdoings, as he called them—for a period of time he had been a card cheat! This desire got hold of me, and every day that passed without seeing him was pure and utter boredom.

Luckily I had so many things to do to keep me busy: furnish the house, buy a couple of new dresses for Olivia—who, funny enough, once she'd walked into a high-end store, agreed to stop wearing the black she'd sworn she'd wear for at least ten years out of mourning—and so the time passed even without him. Finally, when one evening I received a note left with the doorman, who slipped it to me without Olivia seeing, a note signed 'A devout admirer,' my heart—I'm not embarrassed to say it—started to beat so frantically that I was almost ashamed of myself. I actually had to struggle just to calm down. My heart began hammering in my chest the exact same way when I entered his study and saw him waiting for me. He was standing in front of the large window overlooking the Milan rooftops, his beautiful full head of white hair bent slightly to the side, so sweetly it gave the impression that he too, at least on occasion, felt the pain of melancholy—the only trait in those days that indicated intelligence, goodness, and culture. It was only a split second, because his secretary had already announced my arrival: just the time for him to turn around, but for me it was enough to understand vaguely who he was deep down…and also that, if he lost just a few pounds, the man in front of me would have been even more handsome than my father. As soon as he bent to kiss both of my hands—exactly as my father used to do with my mother's beautiful friends—I said this to him without thinking. And he replied: 'If you'd cut out that ridiculous *uncle*, I promise I'll go on a diet starting today. I hate all family nomenclature. That's another reason I didn't get married. And on top of everything, that word makes me seem terribly old.'

'You have a deal, Alessandro! I won't call you uncle anymore, as long as I don't see you putting on weight.'

'Oh, a woman is what I needed! Only a woman—a beautiful one, I mean—can give you any self-discipline. Now, gorgeous, tell me everything, I'm burning with curiosity.'

I don't want to tire you with the practically intoxicating happiness I felt throughout the entire year that our 'hoax' lasted. And I won't go into how it felt to discover what we truly were—not just him, but myself as well... Oh yes, because with him, and only with him, did I start to see what I really wanted. Alessandro lost weight, as he had promised, and thankfully I was no longer supposed to call him uncle. The most beautiful moments were when he would take me somewhere, on a weekday, to give Olivia the impression I was going away for work: Capri, Venice, Vienna, concerts, shows, everything, even places that were already familiar seemed new and fairy-tale-like next to him. It was because of him that I grew so attached to his old friend and business colleague—or a partner in crime, who can say?—the one who would become my husband. His name was Leopoldo, and he worked in the stock market. I first saw him in my uncle's office, and there was such a strong resemblance between the two—not because of their age, Leopoldo was ten years younger, but for their joyfulness in taking on life... At times they even seemed like the same person, or like a double-faced Janus at the very least, despite the differences in their facial features and hair color. Leopoldo had a dirty blond mane, that soft color that veers toward a shade of pink, and which looks as if it could never stand the test of time but actually often lasts into old age.

One thing that made their relationship even more unbelievable in my still somewhat childish mind was the story recounted in two voices of the time when they were down on their luck in some country in the Far East. They decided to become blood brothers, and they performed a ritual: each one pricked a finger and sucked the other's blood. To prove to me that it was true, they showed me a tiny tattoo, usually hidden beneath the large stones on their rings, representing the rotation of the sun, like the one the Nazis adopted."

15

"I really couldn't say when exactly Leopoldo tiptoed into the relationship that had solidified between Alessandro and me. It happened naturally, over time. We were such a harmonious trio, and all eyes would be on us whenever we'd walk into a restaurant or a theater. I believe that's why marriage proposals started to rain down on my head like cherries. Men are always strongly attracted to women accompanied by important men. But I didn't say how Olivia began to go out with us, too. It was so easy in the end to get her to accept that wicked uncle, I nearly forgot to mention it. Leopoldo, dying with curiosity about my little sister, one day shouted to Alessandro, 'She never saw you, as a child, I mean?'

'No.'

'Not even in photographs?'

'Absolutely not! Even the photos had vanished, right, Erica? Plus, I had run away at sixteen.'

'So why don't we go see her, as friends of Erica's? The last name shouldn't be a problem, yours is so common. It won't be hard for you not to call him uncle, Erica, since you never do.'

We gave it a try, and everything went as Leopoldo had predicted. The thing that made us secretly laugh our heads off was that Olivia immediately took to Alessandro, so much so that one day she declared, 'He has the same last name as us—too bad he isn't a relative. He's so sweet and defenseless.'

All of this was also made possible by the fact that Alessandro truly hated familial relations. He didn't tell a soul— besides Leopoldo—that he was my uncle, even if this meant coming across as my lover, something Borletti believes to this day. Since he couldn't stand his old milieu, which was the same as ours, he no longer saw anyone who came even close to knowing us. He had a whole international network, not only of 'dealmakers,' bankers, and industrialists both small and large, but of artists and writers who adored him and awaited him with open arms everywhere from Milan to Paris to New York. It was with him that I discovered modern art and decided to dedicate myself to it. Don't think that I spent my days between theaters and hair salons—this, unfortunately, was the turn that Olivia's life took. As she grew up, she slowly drifted away from Fiore, becoming an exact copy of our mother, only with a warmer temperament, more open and affectionate. I, on the other hand, for whatever reason, did nothing but study, especially the world of markets and finance, following Alessandro's work. This was a great stroke of luck for me. I didn't become a real expert on the stock market—you need an innate talent for that, like to be a poet—but I became so well acquainted with that concrete yet fantastical world that years later I was able to look after the assets my husband left me with some success. If it hadn't been for that, I'd be almost poor today.

The world of business—how many exciting and heinous discoveries! To the outside observer it can seem like a crazy game, but it's not. It's more like a primal battlefield, with its good soldiers, its clashes of bayonets and mortar fire. On more than one occasion when listening to Alessandro and Leopoldo's discussions, I had the clear sensation that they were facing each other off like two real-life swordsmen—that's right!—that the whole atavistic habit of sword fighting, and the desire for physical aggression, had (in this age of ours that many call modern) moved from the arm muscles to the brain—to the imagination. It might seem paradoxical, but for me, business is nothing more than the final frontier of the human will to fight to the last breath, and that's why capitalism is really a natural battlefield. It won't be so easy to overthrow, as you Marxists proclaim. But I don't want to talk about politics, that other battlefield, where even the Church has ended up needing to disavow Jesus Christ in praxis—another Marxist term—in order to survive. Italy, after a twenty-year period of unanimous acceptance, isolation, and media silence, seems to have lost its mind for this novelty of arguing, of choosing one's own personal idea to wear like a badge. And they don't know how much this has all been 'willed' by various strategies taken by America. Living abroad much of the time, I've been able to realize how much Italy, which considers itself liberated, has slipped unwittingly under the heel of just the latest foreigner. And maybe even Europe has, too. We'll have to see. In any case, Italy would be the first to fall into this trap. In England, in France, there's at least some resistance toward—oh, I don't know—Coca-Cola. Their newspapers cover a great deal of international politics, while here they talk of nothing but national trifles, as if America didn't exist, as if our country could, by itself, write its own history in finance, and thereby in politics. It's utterly depressing!

But I by no means want to fall into the trap of convincing you that my way of seeing the world is the only possible way. Trying to get you to agree with me is unavoidable, but I'd hate to ruin our friendship as a result. Even if I express my opinions confidently, I'm not at all confident that I'm right. Who can be all the time? Certainly not me. Right now, as I was talking to you, I felt suspicious of my own ideas, as if I might be completely wrong. Always that old suspicion about myself—namely, that with all the talents nature gave me, I haven't been able to cultivate any one of them in particular. As my father would say, I truly am 'Italian': gifted in music, dance, studying, but without any will to hone a single thing. For years I hated this about myself, but a while ago I came to terms with the way I am, to give some peace of mind to myself and to others. Or I could say that I did it to 'be polite' and not to bother anyone. There you have it, not bothering anyone has always been my aspiration. I don't want to start now, and with you of all people, the first woman that I feel as a true friend."

16

Yes, Erica felt that that strange creature with an even stranger name, whom the spirit of Positano had led her to meet, was exactly the friend she had longed for since childhood. She didn't want to lose her, nor, with her, the completely novel sensation of peace that flooded through her after every confessional meeting. If she had been an only child, everything would have made sense. But having had two sisters, whom she had loved, too ... How to explain that hunger for something else? Maybe it had to do with the role her sisters had quickly forced on her, to be the practical one, the one who'd "take care of everything." A role that, deep down, meant being alone, with no one but herself to count on when she needed to be comforted or helped. That's what it must have been, the "loneliness of the leader." The more Erica thought about it, the more she understood that her very closeness to her sisters—the way they loved her or were protected by her—had in turn led her to want what Fiore and Olivia received from her: understanding and protection. Finally there was someone, and a woman for that matter, who at least understood her.

To whom could she have confessed—with the risk of not being believed, or worse, appearing vain, never satisfied—that she hated her appearance every time her image was thrown back at her in a mirror or a photograph? That was the reason why there were no mirrors in the house, besides that awful contraption in the bathroom. If only she could get rid of it! But where in the world has there ever been a bathroom without mirrors? Well, it would be the height of snobbery, she thought sarcastically, fighting back the repulsion that even now, as she combed her hair, her reflection inspired in her. Was it because she felt undeserving? No, that repugnance had clung to her since childhood. And what was it that calmed her so much after confessing this to her friend, who had done nothing but look and listen, instead of rushing to disagree or to try to make her feel better? A relief that no renowned analyst had been able to give her—she had felt it then and continued to feel it now, more than a year after she'd described the guilt that had nearly driven her mad for years: that she hadn't been able to save Fiore.

Starting with that relief, and thanks to that relief, our friendship deepened, to the point that one day I said to her as we were walking, "I understand you so well, sometimes

GOLIARDA SAPIENZA

I feel like I am you. Do you think it can happen, this transferring of the self to another person?"

To enter into another being, how liberating that would
be! To be nourished by the other, before going back to the
same old self, but renewed. It was the special privilege of
friendship, one that made it perhaps greater than love.
In love there's always the risk of remaining imprisoned
in the other—it's more enthralling, of course, but it's also
dangerous. "The two friends"—to quote the wise old people
of Positano (whom many considered indifferent, but this
wasn't the case)—with time ceased to arouse any amazement: We were so close that, as the summers passed, our
initial nickname was even replaced with "the sisters." In
fact, during one unusually hot September that felt like August, Olivia (it was the first time I'd met her) had such a furious fit of jealousy that all three of us ended up spending
the whole night arguing. After mini-fights, tears, and finally some sighs of resignation on the part of the gorgeous
Olivia, we decided not to go to bed, but to run to the beach
and take her speedboat to Capri to finish the night at one of
the bars, watching the sunrise, before "flying again on that
still, smooth sea to the ends of the earth," as Olivia said
while she started the motor.

"It's probably due to the fact that we weren't allowed
to even raise our voices at home, let alone fight, but last
night's row, Goliarda, erased my feelings of jealousy toward you nearly entirely—I said nearly, don't get ahead of
yourself... I'm jealous with everyone, with my husband,
my daughters, friends... but most of all with Erica. I don't

get jealous of the children or my husband around her, even though she's so much more beautiful than me—not to mention intelligent and cultured. But I know what it is: Erica is so incredibly moral, you can put complete trust in her. Fiore was also that way, but her morality didn't seem so astonishing; she was the most beautiful one of the three of us, such a classic, saintly beauty that you felt being moral must have come easily or naturally to her. But Erica, who's so full of enthusiasm and passion . . . well, you know what I mean—you get the sense that it's a victory over her own nature, and you have to admire that . . . But what were we talking about? My God, is it possible that I can't ever manage to follow a topic to its logical conclusion? Sometimes even I can't stand myself, I swear . . . Fiore, my oldest daughter, says that everyone at school says 'I swear' and also 'hoot' to show real admiration, but I don't like 'hoot' one bit! It must be that it reminds me of 'the stone whistles, hoot and cheer the name,' that horrible Fascist song, and how they'd always say they 'didn't give a hoot' about anything . . . They were so vulgar! It was because of their vulgarity, as my father said, that you couldn't feel like supporting them even if you tried—in our household, I mean. Outside, everyone was Fascist, everyone!"

From Fascism, Olivia goes on to tell me about her father, her mother, her happy childhood, Milan. I know enough about their past, and I can let myself get lost in the contemplation of this woman, who's so similar to the Olivia Erica told me about, and also so different now that I see her naked in the sun. She's magnificent—a *Maja* *desnuda*—sitting on the rock as if it were a comfortable ottoman, her legs crossed, while she curiously gesticulates like an ill-mannered boy. When she arrived in Positano, her skin was the peach color that on some brunettes lasts even through the winter, but in a few days it has acquired a polished, coppery glaze. Her black and wavy raven's hair casts dark shadows in the emerald green of her eyes. Her natural class has saved her full breasts, hips, and thighs from appearing vulgar. Without that ancestral style, perfected over the centuries, Olivia would've been no different from any of the countless chorus girls; or, at best, she would've merely incarnated the *signorina grandi firme*, that hidden ideal of so many boys from the Fascist era.*

Something Olivia says, however, awakens me from these mental meanderings: "Erica's morality is so clear to see, I don't know why I talk about it so much; maybe because of how inferior it makes me feel. But who could say how far she'd go in sacrificing herself for someone she loves? I bet that she didn't tell you about it, and that you didn't even guess either."

"Well, actually..."

"Go on, you can't leave your sentence hanging like that."

"You're right, it's a bad habit of mine. But I don't know if it's right for me to say."

---

* *Le grandi firme* (literal translation: *Big Brands*) was an Italian magazine with covers displaying women drawn in sensual and often comedic poses, in a style largely inspired by American pinups. The magazine was banned by the Fascist government in 1938.

"Oh, sure it is, Erica told me that you know everything about her. It made me jealous, and probably your keeping quiet is purely out of—how to put it?—elegance or something like that. You see, when Alessandro lost everything in the stock market... Clearly it's our family's recurring destiny! I'm not an apprehensive person, but I do get a little scared that it could happen again... Alessandro, who already had some cardiac issues, had a sudden heart attack and died. We found him sitting at his desk with his head on his business papers. It was terrible! He had become a second father to us, what could we do without him? For me, marrying without love was out of the question, the very thought of it caused me to have attacks of hysteria. And so, she was the one, as always, who saved me—poor Erica. Could I ever repay her?"

"How did she do it?"

"She made the greatest sacrifice a woman can make. She married Leopoldo, who had wanted her for some time; he had even talked about it with Alessandro, and apparently had received an angry and definitive no. She married him, and this gave me the time to wait for love... But why don't we go back to the house."

The journey from Punta Campanella to Positano is quite short with the motorboat, and yet in that spatial brevity I witness a metamorphosis in Olivia's behavior. Her limbs, when completely nude amid the solitary rocks, moved with the somewhat coarse gestures that women strangely assume when they're among themselves. Now, at the helm of her modern and rapid vessel, Erica's sister has once again the air of a commanding, dignified lady. As she gives the boat back to Nicola, that demeanor, both modest and sensual at the same time, becomes so natural, it's as if she could never be any other way. Nicola shoots a suspicious and cold glance at her, almost with antipathy or detachment. Or is it fear, that stormy shadow that for a second has clouded the boy's Saracen eyes?

In nearly three years, Nicola has grown to be strong and proud, a pride nourished by the daily meals that the Lucibello household can now afford. Business is going well, but both Nicola and I continue to think the same way "when it comes to women," as we'd confess laughing to each other much later. For the moment, the two of us unwittingly have decided to respect our "goddess's" sister and not to judge her, dodging the woman all the same.

· 17 ·

When Olivia had already left Positano, Erica—direct by nature—exclaimed out of nowhere, "Too bad you're not as crazy about Olivia as she is about you."

"Oh, no, I like her very much." I was sincere, it is possible to like someone who in many ways annoys you. "It's only that I get on better with you. The two of us have more in common, I guess."

"True. But still, I need to ask you to love her if you can, because despite the differences between the two of you, and between me and her, Olivia is affectionate, full of life, 'helping'—can you say that? She doesn't know a thing about getting depressed as we do. If you knew how many times she's saved me!"

These sisters never stopped asserting that the other was the more beautiful of the two, that the other had saved them all on her own. Probably if Fiore had been alive, she would have spoken of Erica and Olivia the same way. But then, was she really dead? Or did she also return like a surge of love in the sunsets, to protect them, or merely to watch over them with her gaze?

I often felt Olivia's silent presence in Erica's stories, saving her from herself when she was overcome by remorse or by one of the many setbacks life enjoyed throwing at her. One of these painful instances was when she'd started to fall in love with someone up in the poetic fog of Milan, a man who unfortunately turned out to be a small-time seducer interested only in pleasure, and in making some money along the way. Following this disappointing discovery, Erica had come to Positano to recover.

"Positano can cure you of anything. It opens your eyes to your past suffering and illuminates your present ones, often saving you from making further mistakes. It's strange, but sometimes I get the impression that this cove protected by the bastion of mountains at its back forces you to look at yourself square in the face, like a 'mirror of truth,' while this vast sea, usually so calm and clear, similarly inspires self-reflection. That's why for decades now couples have arrived here thinking they're happy, only to break up after a few weeks—they'd been living a lie—or, on the other hand, why perpetually lonely people end up finding a companion here. Men who think of themselves as the manliest of men find out they're in love with another guy. It's the same for moral problems, that yearning for truth is universal here. Lorenzo calls Positano love's tomb, and he's right; but often the truth can only come out by going through the total death of what you were before, or what you thought you were. I won't tell you, Goliarda, the details of the brief fling that had upset me this winter, because I've already been here a month, and after a short period of grief—short grief after a short fling—everything feels so trivial, so behind me, it's not worth speaking of. Positano and Olivia cured me."

I feel like I can see her sister sitting on the couch next to her when she says her name, smiling as she looks up a second from her crochet work ("Olivia has filled the place with the most colorful blankets and shawls"). Is it because Erica showed me those shawls and blankets so many times? Or did I see them in a photograph? But, in this house of glass and white walls, there are no photographs, not of the lady of the house, nor of her family.

"You don't like photographs, do you, Erica?"

"No, the same way I don't like naturalism in literature or art. I only love 'the dream.' Photography, in my opinion, has pulverized all possibility for us to dream about our own past, and, as a consequence, to dream of a perfect future. Maybe Olivia blabbed something to you about our family? Her inability to keep quiet is amazing, she feels an innate need to be frank. I quite like it, but sometimes, since human beings don't know how to be objective, she can give people the wrong idea..."

"She only told me that you sacrificed yourself by getting married."

"There, you see? She blows things out of proportion. She describes it as a sacrifice because for her nothing is more important than love, whereas for me it's just another part of the business of living. And my experience this winter with that playboy confirmed as much. I couldn't love anyone else after my love for Riccardo...Maybe it's because, as many people tell me, I'm cold; they've repeated it enough to almost bore me to tears. My husband even went a step further, insinuating that I was maybe a lesbian. In Paris he shoved me into the arms of a friend of his, a woman whose pretty little face was always perfectly done up, though she was a bit bawdy physically. Henriette was her name, a formerly poor girl, a free spirit who was ready to try anything. It was a disaster, except for one thing: it confirmed that Leopoldo's psychological cruelty was more absolute than I had noticed when we first married. But why don't we go back to what Olivia defines as my sacrifice.

My uncle's death was a terrible shock for me. It was almost as bad as when Riccardo left, but it had a different tint to it: whereas then I'd fallen into a sort of anguished slumber, after Alessandro's death my mind felt so furiously active and lucid that I almost couldn't sleep, as if the emotional pain my body had ingested was made of cocaine. I was grieving, but this time my grief was full of hate, rebelliousness, and a desire to take revenge—I didn't know against whom—for the death of that old man whom for years now I had, to myself, called a father. Yes, even in death he was my real father, eclipsing that other man's face so thoroughly that I almost no longer remember him.

In those six months of insomnia and fury, I was obsessed with the idea that life was persecuting me, and I decided that I at least needed to save Olivia. Even after everything we'd lost, she still loved life, becoming more and more beautiful, and surer of future love.

Yes, in my mind Olivia personified a kind of utopia, as if saving her from the ugliness of life amounted to saving all of the beautiful things in this world, those few good and untainted individuals, a work of art, or—why not?—a place, like a forest from a fire, just as the mayor Sersale saved this town from real estate investors. That's the reason I think so highly of him, he's an honorable man. If only all of us saved something, and not even a whole town the way he did, then it wouldn't even be necessary to utter the word 'revolution,' because it already would have taken place. A peaceful revolution. But for that to happen, everyone would need to sacrifice something, and I, for my own ideal, did just that. It was easy because, at least for me, life's greater plan—the dream, a utopia, however you want to put it—is realer than the day-to-day. As I mentioned, Leopoldo seemed so similar to my 'father' that making him happy and living with him felt like the continuation of the golden age I'd lived through with Alessandro. Leopoldo hadn't been mixed up in that financial disaster, and he'd always say that my uncle should have listened to him.

Everything went pretty well in the first months of marriage, maybe because we were traveling all around the planet. During that 'honeymoon'—what a stupid word—he didn't pester me with excessive demands for sex, and his enthusiasm for the whole spectacle of the world confirmed that I hadn't been totally off my rocker in thinking that he and his friend were so similar. But as soon as we went back to our normal life, I asked to take part in his affairs, as I'd done with the three of us before my uncle's death. Right then and there, he said—not impolitely, but with a tone I had never heard before, decisive and cold like a steel blade: 'It's unseemly for a man to have his wife always in his hair.' That's the exact expression he used, and the most chilling part was that he said it with the sweetest smile on his beautiful mouth, which was perhaps slightly too thin, always concealed by a reddish-blond mustache and by the glistening of his perfect teeth.

I couldn't respond, I was so taken aback. Meanwhile, he went on saying how I had my collection of paintings, and my Olivia, et cetera. I stood up, and for the first time in my life I went to vomit in the bathroom. You might think that my reaction was over the top, so did I at the time. But afterward, I had to admit that I had caught a glimpse of all the horror that was to come."

· 18 ·

"*Less than a year* had passed since our wedding when I became pregnant, just like my mother had and, going by what she said, all of the women in our family. I was ecstatic, this meant that like my mother I could have lots of children. Maybe I didn't tell you, but I really love children. Silly with enthusiasm, I shared the news with Leopoldo. I then ran up against something so devastating that to this day I find it difficult to talk about. Without even trying to conceal his own displeasure, he said: 'Already? Good to know. In the future I'll make sure myself that we take better precautions. For now, I'll ask you to go to a doctor and fix the situation. I have zero intention of having children, and zero intention of always having them in my hair.'

You can imagine how I felt. I tried as hard as I could to convince him. Like an idiot I reminded him that my uncle loved children and that his only regret about not getting married was that it had prevented him from having kids. His answer made my blood run cold: 'Sure! Alessandro, like all fags'—those were his exact words—'had gotten exaggerated ideas into his head about the joys of having children.'

I won't tell you anything else: the bitterness, the pain was so great I decided I'd run away with my baby. But Olivia, to whom I'd told everything in the hope of having her as an accomplice, simply burst into tears, the poor thing. She was so crushed that I was persuaded to forget about my plan. She was already engaged, and happy, and Leopoldo had put together a dowry worthy of a princess. Oh, as far as money was concerned, he was more than generous, especially if he could bestow it publicly. And besides, she said, we were young and I could have other kids later.

While she spoke everything sounded fair, especially because after initially finding out the news, the idea of having a child with that man started to disgust me. It's awful to say, but how can you have a child with a man you detest? I had an abortion. I'm not sure if it was on account of those doctors in Switzerland or some fault of my own—I had incorrectly counted the months, they said—but, sadly, things didn't go as planned, and they said I could no longer have children. Never again! I was in agony, but the whole thing also taught me a lesson: you can't go against nature without there being consequences, not even once in your life. I had married that man out of self-interest, I didn't love him, or maybe self-interest had made him appear to be something he wasn't. Either way, it could only lead to criminal consequences. I had sold my soul to the devil, without even realizing it. That's how the devil buys you, not with some clear-cut deal. He acts unconsciously, because it's inside of us, evil is.

From that day on, my goal was to come up with a way to take back my soul and my health. Could it be done? Had anyone ever managed before? I wanted to try at least, and as a first step I stopped having intimate relations with that man. On the outside he didn't seem to mind too much, though only on the outside. Then, as soon as Olivia was married and came into possession of the dowry, I left for New York, where I'd made a lot of friends through all the paintings I'd bought. Oh, at least in that respect I hadn't been naive: I had registered the art under my name instead of his, even if, as I said, he was generous in his own way. After a single dreadful year of work, meetings, constant flights between the States and Paris and Milan, I was now going to open a gallery in New York and another one in Milan. Success in business, like in gambling, smiles on those who are unlucky in love . . ."

As soon as she has said these words, Erica goes quiet, turning as pale as a ghost. She looks made of wax, I think, though without any real concern for her—it's not the first time it's happened. She always feels bad about everything, from when she uses the wrong amount of tea leaves to when she takes an overly harsh tone with the servants. Funny thing is, she feels just as bad about these trifles as she does about important matters. Perhaps it's the only flaw this woman has, at least for anyone who stays close to her.

She stands up to walk around the room in a circle, as if to let her negative feelings out physically. Then she sits back down and stares at me feverishly.

"I'm unbearable, I know—and, worst of all, I'm unbearable essentially only with the people I care about most. I was unbearable with Leopoldo too. But why did I paint him as such a monster to you? It's really cowardly of me. I accentuated his negative qualities while skimming over the positive ones, which he had like everyone else, although I was never able to bring them out of him. Actually, I pushed him to develop the worst parts of himself. I'd spotted a diabolic side to him—as if we didn't all have an inner devil—and then did nothing but provoke it, feed it, hoping that it would come out fully in the light of day. It partially comes down to my character and, no doubt, to how we were stupidly taught always to seek perfection... I'm becoming pedantic, I always do when I feel guilty. What I want to tell you is that he only became cruel with me when he understood—and he did quite early on—that I couldn't love him physically. It was astounding to me how important the physical was to him. Olivia is that way, too. I know what you're thinking: Alessandro was also like that. Do you see how unfair I am? I value her physicality along with my uncle's, whereas with Leopoldo... In my defense, being madly in love with me as he was, he wanted me all the time, and there's no torture like having to go to bed with someone you're not attracted to.

With his love for the physical, and the consequent care he took of his body, that personal instrument of pleasure, the last thing I could have expected was him falling so seriously ill, especially at such a young age. At the end of the day he was only fifty-two.

When I received the telegram from his secretary in New York, I almost thought it was a bad joke. But the moment I walked into his room, I understood: not only had what he'd feared taken place—he always said that a bad heart was one of the professional maladies of betting on the stock market—but it had happened in the worst possible way for a human being. He was paralyzed from the waist down, and, worse still, after a couple of months spent in a fog, he regained complete mental control, besides his tongue getting a bit tied between his teeth when he spoke, which soon developed into a stutter. It was frightening to see that large, powerful body motionless like a fallen tree trunk, his head intact with his almost pink hair, by contrast, looking brighter and more vigorous than before, his eyes alive and moving, and his teeth . . .

After six months of this horrible display—I never would have abandoned him—I remembered with terror that I needed to keep a promise that he had coaxed out of me during our honeymoon. He'd told me: 'I didn't marry you just because I love you, but out of selfishness too. So we're even, and now you can cut out repeating it to me every second. You see, the only thing I'm afraid of in life is physical decay—even more so, any mental impairment that could make it impossible for me to put an end to things. I had a friend, more like a brother—no, not your uncle—and we made a pact that we'd each come to the other's rescue in the event of a tragedy. Unfortunately, he died a few months before Alessandro, in a plane crash. So I want you to take my friend's place in the agreement, since he can no longer keep it. In return, I'll leave you everything. I've kept my eye on you, you have the courage and moral fiber of a real man. I trust you more than I trusted my friend, who, after all, let me down by dying. And, being a *real man*, you have to promise me that you'll do this for me—in part because, if you don't, I'll have our marriage annulled by the Sacred Rota. It's easy, just takes some money, and I won't leave you a thing. So, you can take it or leave it . . . I'll tell you where you can find the necessary substance. I got it from a doctor over in Calcutta, it's extracted from a cobra's saliva. It causes a kind of heart attack, and even with an autopsy it's very unlikely for it to show up in the results. Just a pinch is all you need, like tobacco or cocaine . . . We can call it that from today on: our cocaine.'

We would always joke about 'our cocaine.' Ah yes, despite everything, we did joke with one another. But why keep telling this story? You've probably already understood everything, like a good novelist, as my father used to say. Being a novelist is completely different from being a writer. To me, for example, Dostoevsky is a novelist, while Kafka isn't, even if many now say that Kafka is greater than his master. To me he seems like—oh, I don't know—a theologian. Who knows why he's all the rage these days . . . Maybe it's the fact that Nazism put into practice what his work prophesied. In his prophecy, however, he was pointing to something even more terrible, something eternal and absolute that will always be part of man.

Anyway, I needed to keep up my end of the bargain. Was I sorry about it? No. And I wasn't even afraid either, because from the moment I saw him in that bed, transformed into a half vegetable but experiencing mental anguish that no tree or rock ever could, a kind of indifference toward everything and everyone seeped into me. I didn't feel anything, not hot nor cold, I didn't perceive light or colors or tastes. But it all happened painlessly, and I had such an active strength that sometimes I felt like a perfect machine in constant motion, propelled by inner workings so finely tuned and oiled they never even made a sound. Silently, I saw myself while I acted, thought, made decisions. And there was no amazement on my part, nor on the part of other people, who all assumed this new attitude of mine was due to profound sorrow and an even more profound sense of duty to my beloved husband. And why wouldn't they? No one suspected anything from our quarrels, which are completely ordinary in our social class, as Lorenzo likes to insinuate—that awful Lorenzo who knows everything, but who in the end doesn't understand a thing, apart from painting. The ones with actual understanding are Giacomino and Pierpaolo, and Wally too, that last, beautiful relic of the Parisian cafés. She's practically becoming a monument to that extraordinary past. The mayor even awarded her a pension, as one does for the survivors of a golden age, and a little house with a small garden, up at the end of the town. She's happy there with her animals, her canvases and filth. The whole town was happy about the decision. Do you remember when the children used to call her Death? Death has arrived! Death in Positano! It feels like yesterday, but six years have already gone by . . .

Sorry for the digression, I should get on with the story of when I turned into an efficient machine, indifferent to the world. But why keep upsetting you with these tales from my life? They might make you sad, whereas for me, having lived through them, they seem mild, like everything that's necessary. That's the difficulty in telling one's life story to others: the painful parts cloud over everything and become too much to take, but it's really not the case. Because even in pain there is life, and pain becomes diluted over time, broken up by moments of perfect happiness, of satisfaction and peace.

But you need to tell everything about yourself at least once, if you're lucky enough to find someone you can trust. No one can keep it all bottled up forever, or else they'd go insane. In fact, I need to thank you: if I hadn't met you, I'd surely be in an insane asylum today. And besides, life is always a novel left unwritten if we leave it buried inside of us, and I believe in literature. Only what's written lasts and over time shapes itself into a life—the only life that's legible, even if seen from countless angles; and, paradoxically, the only one that's absolutely true. This little sermon is directed at you, Goliarda, and the problem you chose to let me in on: devote yourself to the craft of storytelling, don't be intimidated by the destitution that has always plagued those who pursue that art. And don't get sad now. Why is it that every time someone talks about you, you become sad! Are you worried because you're not sure you're a Gertrude Stein? You yourself said that it's better for a woman to write cheap books like Peverelli* than to castrate herself through self-criticism. Let's move away from these categorical abstractions and be practical for once. At least give it a try. And know that this suggestion of mine is not a disinterested one: I might be more of a heroine manquée with all of my shortcomings, but I'm sufficiently narcissistic not to want to disappear completely when I die. Maybe with time, in twenty, thirty years, you'll write about me. Wherever I'll be then, I'd like to come back through your mind, to be seen by others. People don't live for themselves alone, this might be what separates us from animals . . . There you go making one of Iuzza's little scared faces. Give up that nickname and push yourself into the realm of adults—it just might get you somewhere."

---

* Luciana Peverelli (1902–1986) was a prolific writer of popular romance and crime novels who published her first books in the 1930s.

19

My memory grows dark as I think back on that sultry August afternoon full of extreme confessions. What happened after that annoying parenthetical directed at me? The dark of forgetfulness, which is always grayish, full of twisting fog, was wiped away by the dazzling, assured stroke of black varnish of the Positano nights, when everything turns quiet to sense the melodious smells of jasmine and herbs coming from the countless gardens. Even the sea grows silent, overpowered by the incredibly fragrant smells of the Coast.

"I'm sure," Erica says, "that if we took the car and drove around all the way to Vietri, we wouldn't find anything but silence and scents, with only a little excitement coming our way between Vietri and Salerno just to remind us that we're not already underground, finally killed by too much natural perfume... But going back to me and my story, after Leopoldo's illness I spent about five or six months in which, as I said, I divided my time indifferently between him, the doctor, and the business affairs which I was perfectly able to take care of under his guidance. I had forgotten about the death pact he'd sworn me to, and probably never would have considered it if something in his behavior hadn't forced me to dredge it back up. He had given me all of the keys to the safe box, though I was absolutely banned from opening a specific folder inside of it. And this was his big mistake, because if he had never pointed out that folder with the word 'personal' written on it, it never would have piqued my curiosity in the first place.

But that command—the usual mistake made by dictators, who in bossing people around convince themselves they have some supernatural power over others—practically obligated me to take that folder. I brought it into my room, and, in that sleepless night of horrible discoveries, I read how he had been the cause of my uncle's ruin. He hadn't done it out of pure evil, but to save his own skin from past mistakes, dealings that were borderline criminal, connections with strange mafia groups from South America that had built a network in Europe and needed a scapegoat. I should have you read what was in that folder, and I would, but I destroyed it as soon as his eyes were shut for good: keeping it could have proved dangerous for me as well.

The thing that struck me the most, and woke me completely after all my sleepwalking, was not only the cowardly thing he'd done to my uncle, but the absurdity of his saving those documents—it was like catching him red-handed. Was it due to the usual senseless confidence of the dictator, which had been pushed to its apex by his Nietzschean values (or Hegelian, which are really the same thing)? How many times had he said to me that genius can do anything! That's right, he thought of himself as a genius, and he also wanted the documentary proof of that genius put in writing, and never far out of reach. And I must say, in the schemes that unfolded before me as I read, Leopoldo had actually been a genius. My uncle came across playing the role of the *ingénu*, all heart and feeling.

From that moment, I became lost in a rage I'd never felt before—it's terrible, but my entire mind and imagination were filled with a single word: revenge. That despicable word pounded away at my brain like an annoying melody, one that you try in vain to forget, but thanks to its very triteness keeps on playing in your head without end. It was awful, but it didn't last long, no. After two days, as in a horror film sequence, everything came crashing down: the doctor told me that Leopoldo would never recover. After the news—it's ghastly, but I have to say it at this point—like a creditor, I coldly reminded him of the pact. He replied that the pact was from when he'd been healthy and stupid, he was another person now: 'My body has changed, it doesn't weigh on me anymore. I want to live my life. I can still see you, read, listen to music, taste foods. You wouldn't believe, Erica, how much I can taste flavors.'

Oh no!—the refrain kept pounding away inside me like hellish clockwork—oh no, too easy! The first chance I had, I added a bit of that powder to his orange juice and I put an end to things with him, and with me. Yes, with myself as well. All that suffering was immoral, slimy. And hate is slimy, too, a powerful snake strangling you. Sure, what I did was criminal, but, at that point, was my life anything more than an unraveling of criminal ties and compulsions? With that act, I believed with all my heart that I was putting a stop to the diabolic wave that had crashed down and swept away my childhood. Don't they say that every crime ends up being punished in some way? I asked myself this as I looked at a now stone-still head, finally in harmony with his body: the whole thing a perfect statue. That's what gave me solace back then: my confidence that the authorities would find me out and, as was only right, give me the chance to pay for my crime. In order to prove to myself that I was willing to atone for my sins, I did nothing to avoid arousing suspicion, often even feeling tempted to admit to everything. But this would have made it too easy for those who were supposedly the enforcers of the law and of our collective well-being. In my personal fantasy, rather, there was the deep-rooted desire that justice be something sacred, perfect, undeceivable.

Quite early on in the game of chess I thought would take place between me and the authorities, I realized that they had no intention of playing, as they distractedly missed each one of my self-incriminating moves. Because our police are still semi-illiterate, country folk—like most of Italy, for that matter—and my way of playing was too subtle. Or maybe it was due to my ethereal appearance, as the commissioner in charge of the case said to me once, adding: 'Look, Signora, as much as you want to show us that your relationship with your husband was awful, I don't believe it, and all of the servants and your friends don't either. Let it go. You're too hung up over the fact that you bickered like any other couple.'

At that point, I realized that to open their eyes, I needed to show the police the document I had destroyed—either that or I had to give them the details and confess openly. But as I said, it would have been too easy, and most of all I would have been throwing mud onto the names of Alessandro and Olivia, who at the time was happily married and was expecting a child. It's hard to explain my ethical position. I wanted to be held accountable, but only for the one true crime I'd committed: hating the man I'd married.

In just a few days, everything was sorted out in front of my justice-craving eyes. One evening I found myself laughing as though I was actually watching one of those English black comedies, which I'd always thought of as absurd and detached from reality. In fact, they were true. The more the protagonist wanted to be found out, the more she cleared herself and avoided suspicion. Without wanting to, I had committed a perfect crime, and afterward I'd often feel sure that many unpunished crimes had been committed by people like me, in a trancelike state, or merely haunted by some obsessive thought, and not by a professional criminal who'd put years of cunning into carrying out their masterpiece.

But another ethical disappointment was waiting for me around the corner. As the comedy with the police slowly petered out, almost imperceptibly hope began to take root in me, hope for a pure form of remorse, the kind extolled by Tolstoy, Dostoevsky, and the like. That it would rise up so furiously within me, it would give me the strength to turn myself in and finally forget my ridiculous concerns about smearing the names of my uncle, Olivia, and her unborn baby. By now I was alone in the world, that pinch of poison had isolated me from everyone else. A crime leads to solitude, partly from the fact that it's morally impossible to share with others. Alone with my crime, which constantly presented me with my own death, I observed myself and waited for the black cat of guilt to pounce, with its power to make the hammering of the heart as audible as the ringing of a church bell. But none of any of that happened in me. On the contrary, something that would have been unthinkable only a year before took place inside of my body, slowly but tenaciously countering my entire cultural and fanciful worldview, and my moral and spiritual desires.

Gradually, as the months passed, my body began to delight in everything, as if devoid of mind. It was as if I had entered into a new life, or rather, a new adolescence. I was shocked, and for some time I chased after my own pleasure—which had been all but lost—while watching a sunset or taking a walk, savoring a dish or a fruit. Every taste, every smell,

GOLIARDA SAPIENZA

even the basest functions of my body started to give me a
crazed sense of joy. And when, during Olivia's delivery—she
gave birth at home and wanted me there with her—I saw that
small thing, battered yet vigorous, come out almost miraculously from that other, fully grown and powerful body, a
feeling of joy like never before ran through me. I yelled and
cried so loud I frightened the obstetrician. Olivia, rather
than suffering through childbirth, had completely taken the
reins, 'like a simple country girl,' to use the obstetrician's
words. I think she laughed along with me, I can't remember—I only know that she called me close to her and hugged
me tightly, whispering, 'Listen to her crying. She's born!
She's healthy. We did it, my dear sister, we did it!'

From that snowy dawn, where the sky and the earth
were one single pearly surface, I no longer worried about
myself, about my past and my future. Olivia in that crown-
ing moment had joined me to her in the joy of bringing
that baby into the world: 'We did it,' she had yelled, and
the phrase echoed in me like a hymn of victory, of life over
death—the very thing that seemed to have taken over our
destiny for the last ten years.

I should maybe feel ashamed of the way I felt back then.
I know you'll think it's over the top, but I don't have any intention, while retracing my past with you, to manipulate
or censor my actions, or to make them seem more logical.
Maybe life can be reduced to a few moral schemas, or to
the 'good tastes' dictated by art and by the penal code? In
any case, another lesson was made overtly clear to me that
morning: just how powerful and illogical that life-giving

force is that pulses through us and through all of nature. And, bowing my head before the glaring imperfection of the universe, I lost God. Or, who knows, maybe I lost that perfect, metaphysical God I'd sought for years, and caught a glimpse of that barefoot, human God who walks constantly by our side, mangling his feet through the rocks, the thorns, and the scalding sand of this desert we call earth.

By mutual, tacit agreement, Olivia and I decided to name this little child Fiore. And today, this new Fiore, aware of the first one's mistake, is growing up by our side to be strong, intelligent, and healthy—a true source of joy. There are three of us once again, and it's no coincidence that when we're out many people think she's our little sister. After Fiore's rebirth, I felt perfectly happy. Or at peace? Who knows the demarcation point, the border separating the realms of these two feelings? I prefer to say at peace, in any case, and I focused entirely on protecting this peacefulness, even if it meant turning down all the heaps of money that my lawyers—I'd inherited them along with Leopoldo's assets—kept suggesting I could make with lustful and fawning eyes. You can't imagine the effort it took to resist that lust for money. I said no to all of their obscure dealings, which simply left on their own would have yielded immense fortunes; but I knew that they could also lead to great misfortune. Money and business, when set up solidly, as Leopoldo had done, take on a life of their own.

To general dismay, I made do with transferring that entire unholy empire into Swiss bank accounts, living off the income like a coward, as every financial wolf or hero would describe my withdrawal into the sidelines. For them it would have meant poverty; for me it was true wealth and freedom. Olivia's husband was more than well off. And as for me, beyond buying paintings and living lavishly, what could I wish for? You won't believe it, but it took years of exceptional skill to get rid of that empire, like a war strategist trying to pull back from battle with minimal losses. While leading this retreat, I met a wonderful young man who helped me enormously. We had a curious love story, a new kind for me, a kind I hadn't read about in novels, nor heard about from anyone.

During that happy relationship, which mixed passion and friendship, with him I understood that Leopoldo had been right when he accused me of being cold. If I had been that way before, Marco cured me, and maybe, following the early days of passion, I would have married him and spent the rest of my life with him. But Marco wanted children, and, as I told you, I couldn't have them anymore. I underwent some pretty unpleasant surgeries, but nothing could be done. I tried to convince him to adopt, but this didn't figure in with his life's purpose: he came from simple people, and had a Greek mother, magnificent in her natural, Mediterranean ways—she and I stayed close friends—and the idea of not reproducing scared him as if it amounted to the suicide of his entire race. Now Marco has three children. Irene, his mother, sent me pictures of them. She insists that her oldest grandchild resembles me. The power of dreams! Irene never accepted losing me. Maybe it's partly due to the fact that I was rich, but, as my uncle used to say, doesn't richness, over time, become another quality of the person who possesses it? In her own way, she includes me in the continuing of 'their blood,' as the inhabitants of those happy islands call their offspring.

I go to see them in the summer when I can. Last year, I took out all of them along with my niece, Fiore, on a rented gulet, and we made it to Turkey. Mightn't they be a bit my children, too, in some way?

If it weren't so boring to listen to others talk about their children, I would go on for hours, telling you everything about them. They're wonderful. And the most fun thing of all is that this past winter, Fiore revealed to me that she's in love with Nikolas, the oldest, but she doesn't want to confess to him because she also likes Andreas and she wants to take her time. Children and their endless dreams. The enchanting, boundless space that is their days. Their magnificent way of 'believing' that they are the first and last protagonists in all of creation, that they're immortal. It's a shame that at a certain point their time has to be divided, or, I should say, reduced—that first heinous act of oppression—into hours, weeks, months, years, clocks, history, identity cards. Such a shame! Oh, Goliarda, let's also forget for a few hours our 'adultness' and pretend to be children. The clock tells me it's midnight, but I'm hungry. Clearly confessing works up an appetite. And I feel like spaghetti. Come on, let's go cook some. After, we'll speed along the coast, listening to the timeless silence emanating from those mountains which were hurled down by some god of chaos, in a rage against all that is order."

20

After that night spent racing through the dark—at certain points at the bends in the road I almost felt that the car was levitating over the cuts in the cliffside, pulling us upward in a sensation of upside-down vertigo—we started to keep a silent dialogue going, even at a distance, while we each separately faced that "other life," or the "trench warfare" as we called it, which beyond planet-Positano raged more and more as peace solidified throughout Italy and Europe. A telegram, a quick phone call, or a silly postcard could act as a lighthouse over the crushing waves of daily life.

At the beginning of the summer of 1958— exactly ten years after our first meeting and three from that famous drunken night full of confessions, silences, and fragrances—I received a huge postcard from New York with a nighttime view of Manhattan. (We had started a "bad taste" competition between the two of us, which consisted in hunting down the very worst that means of communication had to offer, from the antique to the modern.) On it, the minute, precise, and somewhat ostentatiously antiquated handwriting of that snob Erica proclaimed: "I'll be expecting you in Positano in July. I'm happy! And I want you to meet the reason for my happiness. I feel like I've been blessed by a miracle. Consider me blessed!"

My Erica is in love, I think as I run down the stairs in Positano to meet her at Giacomino's café, where we'd always meet right after setting foot in the enchanted town, as if ritually continuing our first meeting. No one dies in this town, except when they've already lived to be a hundred, and then only because they're tired of living—like Giacomino's father, who made it to one hundred and five, or the tobacco shop owner, who's also close to living a century.

Entering into the tranquil shade of that café–pastry shop which constantly smells of sugared candies, I spot Giacomino. He's still in one piece—he was already old when I met him for the first time. He flares his smile, like a mischievous boy at your service, under a blue beret lightly dusted with flour or the angelic powder that's always floating in his mythical, timeless bakery.

By the way that sorcerer of tastes greets me, it seems like we haven't seen each other for only a few hours, instead of a long winter. Then he says: "Your friend is on the veranda. She's waiting for you. She seems to be doing well, Erica, really well, and I'm happy for her. What would you like, the usual baba and tea? Or with the heat this morning, would you prefer a peach granita?"

For a year, Giacomino, by unwittingly imitating Frank Lloyd Wright, has managed to amplify his little place in the sky's direction. He swapped the small windows for ones that run floor to ceiling, and planted sturdy wooden poles amid the plants in the large orange orchard; then on top of them he laid a deck covered in asymmetrical holes out of which the vigorous orange trees can rise up, casting the tables in the shadow of their leafy crowns.

Having passed through the French doors, I feel as if I'm on the deck of a ship sailing on a dreamlike sea, and I realize that the baker's know-how in utilizing spaces comes from his experience as a sailor. Distracted by this revelation, I almost don't recognize Erica on the other side of the deck. Behind splashes of the green, frothy leaves, she is silently gesturing at me to come over, since it's prohibited on that ship to disturb the other passengers enjoying the calm sailing.

When I finally notice her, another revelation stops me so abruptly on that ship's deck that I almost feel dizzy with actual seasickness. Maybe the wind has picked up, I think. But as soon as I get closer, I realize that the waves that just sent me rocking were caused by Erica's appearance: unrecognizable.

As if sensing my uneasiness, she stands up and walks toward me, her arms open. In her embrace, everything becomes clear. Erica has truly changed, and that's not all;

it's the first time she has hugged me, and it is so warm and full an embrace that it transforms my seasickness into a knot of distress, as if for an imminent loss. Nonsense, I tell myself immediately as I let myself go in that hug. I was expecting the usual Erica, who's affectionate, yes, but also formal, and that warmth, that bodily openness, that new light on her skin and in her eyes, all of it has caught me off guard. I'm jealous, it's clear that this metamorphosis is due to the presence of a tall man who, in the meantime, has stood up and is now smiling patiently, waiting for the out-pouring of emotion between the two women to end.

I'm only jealous, I tell myself again as I break away from Erica's embrace in order to meet this person. As often happens to me, I don't pick up his name during the intro-ductions. My quick analysis of my own emotions finds further confirmation in his looks: he's charming, beyond any verbal or written description. When his beauty—which is not like a movie star's, but secretive, a coherence of the physical and the soul—comes through in his voice too, my feeling of loss becomes justified. It's clear that Erica will now be all his. And maybe it's because of this—no, *definitely* because of this—that my friend was so affectionate with me. She was overcompensating, trying to ease the pain of our imminent breaking apart.

But who is he? He could be an artist or an intellec-tual, sporting a well-fitted but worn jacket with stretched pockets, filling his little pipe methodically while he hap-pily observes—though not without a hint of irony—the two women displaying their affection in front of him.

"No, he's not English, Goliarda. For once your intuition hasn't hit the bull's-eye, but you almost got the profession. He actually taught for twenty years in California... You know, Riccardo, one of the games Goliarda and I play is we sit at the Buca di Bacco and try to figure out who people are by observing them. She was the one to teach it to me, she says they used to play it at her house. She had an incredible family. Her father initiated her into that game. It was very useful, he said, for understanding 'the human animal.' It's fun, and even educational. I go with Fiore to the café in the Milan train station, and she's also picked up loads from it."

I think: Erica often spoke of a Riccardo. But life can't resemble a novel so blatantly, and the words "it can't be" slip from my mouth.

"Attagirl! I knew you'd get it eventually. It's him, my first love. Not my only one, Riccardo, don't get too full of yourself."

"It's incredible! But how did you two find each other again? Did he look for you, or..."

Why am I talking so much? To hide my jealousy, or is it because I find Riccardo intimidating? It's always hard for a woman to accept that she finds a man intimidating.

Probably I have wandered so far with my thoughts that I almost don't hear Erica saying to her Riccardo: "Oh, don't mind her, Goliarda is like that. At a certain point she goes off with her imagination and you just have to wait for her to come back—if she does come back. Once she drifted off right in the middle of a conversation and I didn't see her again until the following year."

Riccardo laughs. It's his boyish laugh—surprising from such a calm and composed man—that brings me back to my senses and forces me to look at him closely.

"Well, I find it extremely endearing. Sometimes I also get caught up in distractions, in breaks from the present even, but I stop myself because my moral hang-ups won't allow it. I admire you, Goliarda, since you're free enough to act on them. But please, tell me: when you feel tempted to leave the present, is it due to a sudden need for freedom, or is it a means of escaping something or someone you don't like?"

"For me it's both of those things, I think..."

"And in this case?"

"Oh, I only wanted to get away from you, since you're stealing my Erica from me. I'm a very jealous person, and worst of all, I'm jealous in an abstract sense."

"*Adorable!*" He says this word three times, in English, and slowly too, while he stares the object of his admiration in the eyes. It sounds so elegantly decisive—a call for an alliance, or a show of appreciation or approval of his beloved's friendship with this other woman?—that it makes all three of us go silent; not an embarrassed silence, though one strangely charged with emotion, similar perhaps to the signing of a peace treaty between two generals who were enemies until a few seconds earlier.

"You haven't told me how you found each other though."

"Oh, out of pure chance!" Riccardo responds with a changed voice, shriller than before—on account of the signing of the treaty?

"You see, Goliarda, after my divorce—yes, as Erica must have told you, I was married... But I want to gain a sense of freedom and shake off my modesty as you do, maybe it's the first and last chance I'll get. Anyway, my marriage was a disaster, not because of my wife, nor, I believe, because of me. If anything, it was due to something that men used to consider a personal failing: not earning enough money. Sure, both of us worked, but Los Angeles is so expensive... and Ivy wanted a lot of children. It wasn't possible for us, not that ours was a life of poverty, but it was hard-earned. We could afford very few trips—and Ivy loved to travel—few books and records; to put it shortly, we lived in that state of wanting that in the long run becomes worse than poverty itself. A dignified wanting, but without any tragedy, and the greatness that can always be found in tragedy. There was also the pitiful burden of not being able to declare it openly. How to express it? And how not to feel ashamed? But it's the system—America counts on this silence on the part of its wonderful professors while inspiring the world's admiration.

"I have to admit, there must have been something deep between Ivy and me, because in spite of everything we stayed together for a long time. But no love can last in a state of wanting; I knew it in theory, but I couldn't imagine how true it was in practice. Sure, maybe with two heroes, but neither Ivy nor I could fit that description.

"With my marriage over, I decided to leave that university swarming with fierce golden children impervious to all influence, and I ran off to New York. In America, when you want to run away, that's where you go. And I must say that in New York, doing every sort of odd job, I earned more than in Los Angeles . . . I could even buy myself some canvases . . . New York, center of the world, the new Athens, the great bazaar where you can do anything and meet anyone. And as far as finding Erica goes . . . Well, I'd heard that she'd gotten rich, and this very thing stopped me from looking for her. Then one evening at the house of some friends in the Village, I saw her from afar—miraculously identical to how I remembered her. I tried to run away. That's the power of ingrained moralism, which is also foolish pride, narcissism: it even makes you run from happiness. But New York can make the impossible happen, and it made Erica turn in my direction."

"I had felt your eyes on me, your presence."

"The same old romantic from my childhood . . . Did she tell you, Goliarda, that as a girl she wanted to adorn me in her colors like a medieval princess?"

"Romantic or not, now I feel like going to the water," Erica exclaims, jumping rapidly to her feet, a rapidness that's new to her, like a slightly spoiled little girl. Probably the reference to her power as the lady of the castle has re-awakened the joy of exercising that power over the person she loves.

Once we arrive at the bay (a bit more crowded than usual, and it's not even Sunday), I start walking on my own to my boat, knowing the routine. But then Erica hugs me again and orders: "Goliarda, come with us . . . Go by myself? Me? Oh, please! I'm begging you, I'm so happy with the two of you."

"Don't disappoint our princess of the castle, Goliarda," Riccardo adds, laughing. "Princesses, we all know, can't go around without their special lady-in-waiting."

"Goliarda, a lady-in-waiting!? What in the world are you saying? I'll forgive you only because you don't really know her. Goliarda will be my second knight, if not my first!"

"Interesting."

This change in her routine leaves me stunned, but only for the little time it takes to get into the boat (brought to shore by a stranger—where is Nicola?). Once we're out on the water, the barrage of memories they swap between the two of them is astounding, and it supplies all of the questions that have been running through my head for hours with a set of answers. When Erica's with him, it's like she's alone; maybe more blissfully alone than before, the resemblance between her and that aged boy is so stark— even in his smooth, young body, which now stands slender against the backdrop of flaming rocks where they've decided to dock and go swimming. The same gesticulations, the same way of sprawling in the sun as they listen to each other . . . Oddly enough, I amuse myself by thinking that they're siblings, if not twins, and as I recall the saying from my childhood ("birds of a feather . . ."), I conclude that they couldn't have *not* found each other again.

"What are you laughing about, all alone, Iuzza?"

"Oh, I was just remembering Nicola Lucibello."

"Nicola isn't here, he left for military service . . . How the time flies . . . Is that why you're laughing?"

"No, Erica, I'm laughing out of happiness for him."

"Happiness because he's a soldier?"

"It's just lucky for him he didn't see you with Riccardo. His heart would have burst if he'd seen you two together."

Riccardo, even if one gets the impression watching the two of them that he has always been by Erica's side, does not know about Nicola and his love for her, and so he needs to be filled in. She starts with Nicola, but following the rules of free association—particularly powerful among three people peacefully taking in the sun and the silence—Erica transitions into the many stories concerning the locals. I already know how they go, and so I can savor her voice, which doesn't disturb the silence, but enhances it, like the flapping of a gull's wings or the shifting of pebbles pulled by the waves.

"Alfonso is making tons of money, and he intends to open a restaurant on the little beach in San Pietro, using the big boat he bought from Lucibello to shuttle customers. Do you remember, Goliarda, that old, ramshackle, Middle Eastern–looking boat he would use to pick up the passengers coming off the ships from Naples? And so that buccaneer Alfonso has managed to make his dream a reality: his wife, the American girl, doesn't have to work anymore, and he's gotten her pregnant for the third time. I saw her this winter. She was so proud of her big belly! She pushed it out while she walked, to show it off to everyone. It seems like she's become a real local Neapolitan! If it weren't for her canvas-colored hair and her freckles, no one would guess she came from an excellent school. It's the power of this whole Kingdom of Naples—it lets itself be taken over by foreigners, pretending to accept all of their laws, but in a mysterious way it reshapes these conquerors until they're exactly the same as the locals."

"Like China. Erica, you remember the stories we heard from Nonno Cesare, from when he was an ambassador to China?"

"Another incredible thing is that Giacomino's wife has also gotten pregnant. She thought she was going through menopause, but surprise! And even though his wife was embarrassed for what their older children would say, Giacomino was completely against her having an abortion. I asked him why he wanted this child so badly. Do you know what he told me? 'It's not that I want this particular one so much, but no tree should be cut down when it's only about to sprout.' The funny part of the story is that as soon as the news spread throughout the town, the men of Giacomino's generation—fifty, sixty years old? it's impossible to figure out people's age here—took it as a challenge, and they're trying—in vain, it seems—to emulate him. All of them want a baby! Even the parish priest, or at least that's what that malicious Filiberto told me . . .

"That's right, Goliarda, our dear Oblomov of the Coast. But the days of indolent Oblomovism are over for Filiberto, you'll see for yourself when you meet him again. The old bachelor has succumbed, fallen in love with a not particularly young woman from Vienna, once again during the winter—all the things that happened this winter, and not just to me. He's set on marrying her. She's delightful, lively, but what a shift in gears! Poor Filiberto! He claims he's happy, but sometimes he has a kind of worried look in his eyes, like a bird in a cage. You'll have to tell me what you think. Will he possibly be able to stand all of the changes that little Viennese woman is bringing about in his life? If so, it must be true that love can perform miracles. She fixed up the entire building, probably chirping a waltz as she did, and turned it into a delightful little hotel, which was already packed in March with her fellow Austrians. Then she pulled some strings so that the permit Filiberto's father obtained thirty years ago would still be considered valid. They're already building some cabanas for a new establishment by the marina. Poor Filiberto has to watch over the work from sunrise to sunset, and later he'll have to manage everything himself. Can you imagine? Filiberto, who used to think only about card games and the stars, now gets up before dawn. Had anyone ever seen him at the Piazzetta dei Leoni before noon? And yet it's the truth. He even shaves every morning—and the nice shirts his wife bought and keeps tidy for him! Of course, his nighttime friends are furious and keep making fun of him. It seems they've decided to have a kind of strike in opposition to the 'Viennese woman'—that's how they refer to her—and not only do they not say hi to her, but when they see her they turn their backs, which is practically an act of guerrilla warfare in such a mild-mannered town..."

From these stories, Erica goes on to introduce the new arrival to all of the most secret corners of the Coast. Is there anything more exhilarating than seeing once again places, beaches, remote nooks painstakingly discovered, with someone new, reigniting the amazement you yourself felt the first time?

On that crystal-clear afternoon, only slightly undercut by the quiet melancholy of the end of summer, that motionless trio rested on the top of Ravello, not daring to speak or move, the immensity of the space around them inspiring a religious deference. Being perhaps the least inclined to give in to emotions, at a certain point I turn to escape that excessive beauty, and start to head back. I see that Riccardo, whom by now I call "Riccardo the Inflexible" to myself, is crying with actual tears in his eyes.

He must have realized he's been found out, because as soon as I walk past him he quickly turns, practically chasing after me. He calls Erica, who, oblivious in her happiness, soon runs after us like a little girl.

Following that first day, Riccardo and I make a habit of taking a walk together right after lunch while Erica naps. Neither of us feels the need to rest, and so we now find ourselves walking, just the two of us—as we've done for the past month—through the shadowy pathways of Ravello, shadows that always smell of incense, Riccardo observes, still dumbfounded by the fact that this mystical oasis exists in such a carnal, hedonistic context.

"Sometimes, Goliarda, in Positano I almost feel like I've walked into the middle of some wild bacchanal. That morning when tears came to my eyes, it was because I'd been freed. I feel more at home in Ravello . . . What, New York? No, go there and you'll see: New York is not at all materialistic. It's a religious city, in its own way...And yes, it might be Caput Mundi for the money god, but it's still a place of worship, fiery and fervent, but also engaged, ethical. Not like this spiritual and physical wallowing in an oily sea of lasciviousness. Even the mountains—it's unbelievable—they seem like voluptuous bodies awaiting furious intercourse, protruding breasts, wide-open thighs, backs lying on the sand, waiting to be caressed. But don't think that my minor uneasiness will get in the way of Erica's love for Positano. I'm old and I've learned to re-spect others, a sufficient amount at least...And, believe it or not, in spite of myself I'm finding that all of these lush forms and colors are helpful for my painting. The eternal contradiction of the soul: the less comfortable I feel in a place, the more ideas come to me. Yesterday I finished a painting that wasn't half bad, I'll show it to you. And be-sides, how could I allow myself to disturb Erica's peace of mind after she has given me everything, from canvases and paints to the thing I chased after in vain for years, something even more precious: time. The truth is that in this day and age, real wealth is having time, and now I have it in abundance...Yes, I'm a moralist, but, strangely, not in this case; I don't mind being financially supported by Erica. I know that my work will bear fruit over time, and that's one reason I work so relentlessly, as you've seen. The more I work, the surer I am that one day I'll be able to repay Erica for the help she gives me now."

In fact, regardless of how late he was up with friends the night before, every morning Riccardo gets up at six and paints until eleven. Then he punctually joins us by the boat for our daily expedition in search of rocky nooks, beaches, and trattorias hidden in the most unthinkable and secret parts of this corner of the planet which, despite being barely visible on the map, stretches out in front of the bow of our boat like a land without end.

21

That summer, which was without excessive heat or mugginess, astounded even the locals— the older ones saying that they hadn't had one like that in forty years. It did not even hint at wanting to end. This was almost a cause of distress for the threesome—as all of Positano referred to Erica, Goliarda, and Riccardo—since they were the ones who needed to decide that autumn was around the corner, and that they should leave that unending procession of perfect skies and calm, crystal-line seas which had accompanied conversations, thoughts, and gestures, joining their three personalities in a single, mutual understanding.

"If only there was a storm tonight, it would be easier to leave," Erica sighed, then added: "Although it *is* unpleasant taking the ship from

Positano when it's raining. I remember ten years ago, I almost caught pneumonia on Lucibello's boat going from the docks to where the ship had anchored beyond the bay. I swear I felt like I was crossing the Channel or one of hell's rivers. Especially with Lucibello! When he runs into trouble on the water, he turns into a real-life Charon!"

"Really, the ship stops in Positano even when there's a storm?" Riccardo asks, surprised and with a new voice, resonant and seemingly refreshed. It makes me look at him more closely: he's grown ten years younger, I now notice. I'm happy for the change that has taken place in this man whom I now consider a friend—such a close friend that I'm astonished to remember when I didn't know him, or, more precisely, when he was nothing but a blurry ghost from Erica's childhood.

At this point, after meeting Riccardo, I have proof that all of Erica's stories were true, and that they weren't the product of the all-too-human rewriting of her own past (something nearly all people indulge in, to have the strength to push forward through the cruelty of life). But this thought leads me to the unfortunate conclusion that also the second part of her life story was all true. For a moment, a chill runs from my head to my feet.

"Are you cold? You're shivering, Iuzza. What's the matter?"

"It must have been your wish for storms that's affected our little girl. You need to be more careful around children, Erica..."

Riccardo laughs at this joke, which he's started to make at my expense over the last few days. Who knows why—I've asked myself many times—he finds it so amusing? A paternal need? Nonsense, I tell myself, and that's enough with my third-rate psychoanalysis.

"Nonsense, did you say?"

"Oh, yes, I was only referring to myself. It's that . . . well, for some time I've been tempted to go see a therapist, and to fight off this unsound feeling I talk nonsense to myself."

"My, my—the little one needs a father and a mother. What do you say, Erica? As soon as we're married should we adopt her?"

"Oh, I don't know what I'd give to have a daughter like Iuzza."

"You're getting married?" I hear myself say, without any astonishment.

"Yes, in a few days. That's partly why we need to go back right away to Milan. But in secret. Now only you and Olivia know."

"Look—look how she's calmed down at the thought of us getting married. The little one needs legality . . . She says she's against marriage, civil registry, and the established order, but then—don't get mad, Goliarda—who doesn't need a little legality? It's hard to always go against the grain, without parents, without a husband, without . . . But listen, soon you'll have a mom and pop, and when you grow up, we might even be able to find you a good catch, despite your horribly rebellious character."

"It's such a relief that at least *you* understand me, Riccardo. If you only knew how sick I am of playing the lone revolutionary, and in a time when everything is so nice and predetermined."

All three laugh, in a game that could appear silly to anyone witnessing it. But happiness goes hand in hand with silliness. Whoever is without sin can cast the first stone at that *positanese* trio, carefree and oblivious to a world that, as always, went on committing and perfecting more and more crimes beyond those mountains—a metaphysical boundary between the dream and reality, created for an unknowable reason by some mocking god. Maybe he simply enjoyed occasionally throwing a few scraps of peace to mortals; but only to remind them how happy they could be, and with so little, that way increasing a hundredfold the pain that comes later, upon reawakening.

Waking back up to reality, in fact, was extremely hard for Goliarda. As Lucibello lifted her up, she had no choice but to leave the small pier, before being hurled into that ship which would inevitably take her far away. By the docks Erica and Riccardo wave handkerchiefs in a time-honored gesture, at least since ships started to fill themselves with emigrants. Too bad they're not here with me, Goliarda thinks, then parting wouldn't be as difficult. But Erica has decided at the last minute to take a taxi to Naples and from there an airplane. Every time she has to leave, she begins to panic and delay, sometimes for so long she's eventually forced to take the quickest means possible. Beneath her efficient, confident, and queenlike air, she's also afraid of parting. And why be surprised? It's a peculiar characteristic of queens and great minds, after all—even Freud suffered from it.

Meanwhile, the boat, with a great din of sirens and voices and even some nostalgic Neapolitan music in the background—all of the ships that cut across the islands show these abandonment issues—moves out into the water, scaling the bay of Positano down to what it geographically is: a small fissure lost in the immensity of those colossal cliffs. Once I lose sight of the white flittering of the handkerchiefs, followed by the glimmering Saracen church dome which from afar seems to rest on the silver of the sea, I decide to get a whiskey at the bar. I want none of the melancholy of parting, gripping the railing and watching the mountains recede solemnly into the distance.

In the barroom, instead of the usual few, calm passengers I used to run into until the year before, an excited, boisterous crowd weaves around the handful of already occupied tables. The bar itself is completely overrun, and the old bartender looks flushed, even if he tries to keep moving with the elegant calm of seafaring men, while just barely managing to serve everybody. *What happened?* I ask myself as I stare at my friend. From behind the bar, he makes a forlorn gesture with his arms, which in Neapolitan means: party's over! This is what Giacomino implied even a few years ago, when he'd say: "Enjoy these last years in Positano, because when they're done widening the road, it'll all be over."

Then, in Rome, right outside of the station, where before there had always been two or three taxis waiting sleepily like charmed cats in the sun, a furious whirlwind of cars and a crush of shouting people stops our traveler in her tracks, as if in front of an abyss or the hypnotic gaze of a lurking cobra. How can there have been such an abnormal explosion of cars and foreigners in only three months? Did some malevolent charm keep me in that enchanted planet for decades, while the world changed without my knowing it? No—it's that all phenomena, from wars to genetic and financial mutations to peace, after maturing for a long time underground, pop up suddenly to bear their fruits (edible or poisonous fruits, what difference does it make to nature, which is only fighting to live?), and, at that point, for better or for worse, their development can no longer be stopped. I've seen the flourishing of wars and then of peacetime, and now, cocking my head in front of this new phenomenon, I prepare myself to face the individual war that awaits me in that old Rome which I had come to know as a town, and which—when, yesterday? an hour ago?—has decided to become a metropolis. It's the law of all organisms: continue to grow or perish.

In that war of changes, of new competition, new ways of speaking to assimilate in order not to fall behind—with the ancient town still rooted in my nerves and in my veins—I forgot about Erica, and her life already written

by some anachronistic novelist. By now my friend, se-
cured in her wealth, was sheltered from the catastrophes
that always lie in wait for those who have to earn a living. And she also had a companion to satisfy her hunger
for friendship, the only hunger that can cause even a rich
person to starve.

22

Three years passed in which we didn't see each other. In our defense, I had my work in film, while Erica had her trip around the world, a gift to herself and to Riccardo, followed immediately by his numerous exhibitions. The catalogues arrived punctually at my address, along with the usual ugly postcards with a few jokey sentences from the newlyweds. Riccardo had a show in Rome too, but at the time I wasn't in Italy because of work.

And so I thought Erica's story had quietly concluded with a happy ending, and I delighted in this—the reader in me detested all of those gratuitously tragic finales that writers often use to satisfy their desire to take literary revenge on life.

I was coming back from a walk on an afternoon in April—when birds and trees and people get carried away in a feeling of spring enhanced by the purplish shiver of the wisterias—and I was full of nostalgia for the many other springs spent amid the peaks of the Coast where the wisterias sometimes hold out long enough to meet the furious yellow of the broom trees. Then, in the mailbox, I found a postcard, one that was different from all the others I'd received. It was in black-and-white, with a photo of Piazzetta dei Leoni from the Fascist era. On the steps, standing at attention, was a small band of awkward and spiritless girls, probably hungry, wrapped up in the official uniforms of young Italian females. One of them was giving a Roman salute with a big, beaming smile, unclear whether out of joy or derision. On the back, instead of a hurried greeting, it said: "I need to see you so badly. Come soon, I'll be here for two months and maybe forever. Erica."

My reply was a short telegram dictated over the phone: "Tomorrow afternoon I'll be at Giacomino's as always." Then, feeling no surprise for the joy caused by that postcard, which had led me to settle in just a few hours any obstacles standing in my way, I am running down those steps, once again in that "old carefree time," a time that already feels so far away as to border the realm of childhood memories.

Giacomino is there, in the sweet-smelling shadows, his large golden eyes continually on the alert. His beautiful bishop's hands don't settle for pointing me to where Erica is waiting, but with time-tested friendship and renewed affection slap me on the shoulders as he says, "Go ahead . . . The two of us will talk later."

I'm so happy to be back, I don't notice the worry that has turned the constant glow in the baker's eyes into a dark gold. But when I spot her, my happiness collapses into distress, nearly causing me to turn around. But it's too late. As always, Erica has sensed my arrival, and she has already stood up. Why am I panicking, I wonder—maybe I've missed Erica more than I thought. The feeling is immediately confirmed when I find myself in her arms, crying in a way unbefitting an adult.

I don't realize at first that she too has tears in her eyes. The shoddily disguised surprise of a few customers— Germans? English?—scattered around the tables of the garden-turned-ship's deck brings me back to my senses. When I look up, I calm down completely: Erica has not changed one iota, it's just her tears and that rather grim outfit—made for a lady in mourning?—that have made me feel concerned.

"I really missed you, Erica."

"So did I."

"I didn't know."

"Well, I did. Is that why you're looking at me like you don't know me?"

"No, it's just your dress, I think. I've never seen you in black."

"Oh, I know, it's because of the past three years spent in those gloomy lands of the north. Without realizing it, I was forgetting about colors, but tomorrow I'll throw away this tailleur. Actually, would you come take a look around the stores with me? Or, now that you've published a book, I suppose you have no choice but to look down on shopping?"

Erica cracks this joke as if she's picking things back up after a day or an hour. Friendship has this power of erasing time and distance.

"I'll see if I can take into consideration such a frivolous activity," I respond, thrilled about this sign of our renewed bond. "And where's Riccardo?" I ask, following the timeless rules of the game of friendship, by which one also has to care about a friend's family members, or lover, even when it's not exactly the case.

"Oh, where he always is. He's been working since seven on a new painting, but he'll come at eleven. He's as meticulous as a calculator, and with no hope of jamming or running out of power."

"And how is Olivia? And the girls?"

"She terminated her third pregnancy. And with such a 'modern' spirit, as you and that Pirandello of yours say, that it left me speechless. I'm tired of women! There are already three of us in our family, leaving yours truly out of this category. I can't take it anymore, the bloating, the female pains, that time of the month . . . Right, because Fiore—you do remember her?—she's already all grown up. I don't know about you, but I never found it to be so terrible—a bit troublesome, yes, but completely natural. Maybe it's because, as Fiore says, I've stayed old-fashioned. Times change, Goliarda. I might seem reactionary to you, but I find these changes somewhat stifling. Don't think I judged Olivia for having broken our absurd female tradition: it's no longer a good time to have a lot of children. But that her love for her husband would end so quickly, and in such an ugly way, that really did cause me to suffer . . . How to explain it? My father used to say that when times change—he was referring to the end of the First World War—not only does our way of speaking change, too, but so do sensations, feelings, et cetera. And he was right . . . Actually, sorrow was not what I felt when Olivia told me that she was ending things with Ferdinando, and even if he kicked up a little fuss, he had no intention of opposing her wishes. They got a divorce last spring, I'm not sure in which foreign country . . . But more than anything, I wanted to be able to convey my reaction to you: it wasn't a feeling of sorrow limited to Olivia, her children, and me; it was more like there had been a great defeat—oh, yes—like a war had been lost, a general catastrophe . . . A metaphysical sorrow, that's what it was! I admit that it's excessive, and, even if I know you won't, please don't say what Riccardo always says to me, lecturing me about times changing, and unstoppable progress, and all that. I see that you're not laughing, thankfully. I hope that if you do, you'll laugh at him and not at your friend."

"I'm laughing because of him, in fact, and you know why? That madman thinks he can control what happens because he still has you—and while he lectures you about modernity, he doesn't realize that he only can so long as he relies on your being old-fashioned! I'm not so amazed to hear about Olivia. Also in our circle of married and unmarried couples—relationships that had seemed so solid until three or four years ago—it's been a bloodbath. What's most striking is that in every instance it was the woman who said enough is enough . . . Citto and I were the first. Now I'm the one who needs to ask you not to consider me reactionary, but it was almost as bad as wartime . . . Raimonda, Terry, and other girlfriends of mine in Rome rejoice with every couple that falls by the wayside. A kind of female revolt, savage like all revolts that are overdue. You ask if I'm happy about it? There's something offensive and shameless in this revolt. With their words and actions, they believe they're only harming men, but it's also an insult to women, yelling in that way. But maybe it's fated . . . Oh, here's Riccardo! Erica, you didn't tell me how gorgeous he's become . . . You almost make a girl jealous."

"Was I that ugly before, Goliarda?" Riccardo asks.

"Oh no, never ugly, but too harrowed and gaunt."

"Who knows, maybe it's the power of the materials the painter gets to mix each day. I've discovered over the last few years of work that painting is the closest occupation to being a child that's granted to mortals. Sometimes with the colors, the clay—did you know I started molding? I'd like to start really sculpting after, especially with clay—you feel like you're playing with forbidden materials. It's like going back to a primordial childhood when it must have not been forbidden to play with one's own excrement . . . Anyway, let's go, I don't want to rob Erica of her sea and her sun. She's spent too much time away from it all, and because of me, no less. If you knew what kind of entrepreneurial devil breaks loose in her when she really wants it. A true businessman hides underneath her Botticellian looks. She practically forced my work onto the market in no time. I want to thank you, Erica—only now do I have the courage to thank you. Just like old times, with Goliarda—what did you used to call her, Iuzza?—anyway, with Iuzza, talking comes easy to me . . . Come on, let's go, my little sun-deprived girls. I don't really understand this compulsion of yours, but having realized what you have is a full-blown sickness, I defer to doctor's orders. Not least of all because it affects the two people—will you grant me this, Iuzza?—whom I care about the most."

While walking down the steps, Erica stops, and, giving me a conspiratorial look, heads into a store without saying a word. She then exits wearing an outfit gleaming with color. It must be the colors, or else the sun and air that her body has absorbed in that quick walk; either way, Erica has regained her appearance from when I met her—how long ago doesn't matter—up at the top of the town, when I almost ran her over, rushing around like a movie big shot. Caught up in this memory, I can't help but talk about it. From the story of that first meeting, between the two friends there begins to unfurl a full tapestry of memories before Riccardo, who is silenced, for now, in his role as spectator.

Perhaps they speak so much of the past so as not to see the pretty atrocious changes that have affected even the Amalfi Coast in the last few years. In the narrow, formerly silent and neat streets, a deafening swarm of voices and ungainly limbs staggers along, hampering their barefoot, quintessentially *positanese* pace, which used to make you feel like you were flying. Around the corner that laps against Palazzo Murat like a wellspring, instead of the few paintings and the occasional flower salesman, they see a patchwork of awful canvases and faux-naïf artists, surrounded by gloomy lines of tourists who, sweating and yelling, try to push forward in a hurry. They only have a few hours in this Positano place, now a must-see like Capri's Grotta Azzurra, the Colosseum, the Tower of Pisa . . .

In Piazzetta dei Leoni, the stairway that used to pour out like a majestic delta is jam-packed with people dressed up as old-time inhabitants of Positano; they're so phony-looking, they could be cheap extras hurriedly gathered for a sloppy and pointless film.

The small bay is so full of umbrellas it seems like we've landed in a beach town as popular as Viareggio, and even if Teresa has stayed the same, looking as happy as ever to see her old friends, she's too busy to exchange a word with them. In the boat being brought ashore, the youngest of the Lucibello sons—whom Erica and Goliarda remember as practically a baby wrapped in a blanket, dozing in the shade by the boats—already carries himself as if he owns the place. Nicola isn't there, he's in the north taking care of some business. The absence of that Saracen gaze, and of his cute, forever-enchanted face, make both Erica and

Goliarda silently feel that their youth is over, though without dismay or sorrow, only with a hint of regretful longing. And they could even rejoice in their new stage of life, if they weren't aware of the fact that along with their best years, an entire context of beauty has disappeared too.

Silent now, overwhelmed by the changes that have taken place in their absence, they watch from the old skiff the oozing of cement that flows down from the height of Montepertuso, walling up the old gardens that used to separate the houses and villas like oases of balsamic green.

"We still have this magnificent sea," Erica sighs.

It appears that way from afar, but as soon as they dive in with their masks—it's part of their tradition, Erica going down to collect sea urchins, Goliarda swimming after her with a net—they see a trail of plastic bags strewn along the sea floor, covering the entire sunken amphitheater of Conca dei Marini: a venomous visual vertigo. But it doesn't matter, there's always the immense and serene dome of the sky, seemingly resting on the mountains of jade and amber, and, at night, the bountiful blossoming of stars, so vivid and so close you feel that you could lift up a hand and caress them.

The general decay is kept at the fringes of the happiness they feel at being reunited, partly because the locals—from Giacomino to Ciccillo the Cemetery, or Alfonso the Shark to Filiberto—have all stayed the same.

But when Olivia arrived, as she did every year, for her brief stay in her sister's cherished town, the spell the two friends had falsely kept afloat was broken.

"You two are crazy to stay in this cement pit. It's worse than Milan. Why don't you pack your bags and come to Crete? There you could actually find night skies and a sea like in the old days."

Olivia has also changed so much that her disappointment over the place's decline sounds like hot air. Probably, after the two pregnancies, she was on the verge of becoming matronly, like nearly all of the beautiful dark-haired women of the Mediterranean, and in her effort to return to the slimness of her youth she's only managed to imprison herself as well in the sharp lines—refined, perhaps, but inhuman—of all of those feminine mannequins that fill the pages of *Vogue* and *Harper's Bazaar*.

Riccardo didn't come down that morning, giving the elegant excuse: "I think I'll be in the way of you three friends. I'll leave you girls to your 'mysteries,' even if I'm a tad jealous." Erica doesn't go out either the next morning, probably too sad after her sister's critiques of "her" Positano. Over the phone with me, she blames it on a terrible headache, before making a cryptic request: "Please go boating with Olivia. Try to figure out where all this unhappiness is coming from—it's been tormenting me for almost two years. I've seen that you've also noticed what a morbid state she's in..."

This task probably would have annoyed just about anyone. But I love to get to the bottom of things, and maybe I'm even drawn to the opportunity to be alone with that woman, whom I have loved up to this point as a reflection of my love for my friend, and only now have I started to detest.

At least I'll know why she gets on my nerves so much, I think, and I'll finally find out if it's due to old jealousy, or if it has some foundation in the way Olivia actually is: her self-centeredness, or even her excessive perfection and confidence in how she looks and acts. Despite the complete artificiality of her stylized figure (or maybe precisely because of this), she still is so regal and beautiful that even the sloppy, hurried crowd has to turn to admire her, moving aside to let her through like a diva.

As soon as we're alone on the boat, Olivia takes off all physical and mental accessories—the only expression of her character that has stayed the same in all these years—and lies out in the sun with her legs apart.

"It's so hard to tan the creases in the groin!"

She's grumpy, who knows why or with whom, and she doesn't say a word for at least an hour. Lying on the other side of the boat, reading under a hat the size of an umbrella, I almost forget that she's there. Then suddenly I hear her jump to her feet.

"My God, I'm starving!"

"I think there's some fish and other things in the icebox."

"That stuff makes you fat! Oh, thank goodness—there's an apple."

"And apples don't make you fat?" I ask insincerely, while in my heart I'm laughing, knowing that my diagnosis from the day before was spot-on: Olivia is so mad with everything and everyone because she's always hungry. Who can stay in a good mood while living off only apples and a few leaves of lettuce?

"No, apples, pineapples, those are fine...The food-combining diet...Three days of bananas and skim milk..."

She unloads so much knowledge on the topic of apples that I can't help but be impressed. Putting my book down, I decide to stare more closely at that beautiful woman who in her rambling on protein values and calories has turned into a professional lecturer, or a saint possessed by a sole aspiration: to starve to death in the name of aesthetics.

It's so enjoyable to watch the intensity with which she lets out her energy and those beautiful words that I almost don't realize it when, at a certain point, she has already changed topics. Hurriedly, I ask, "Sorry, Olivia, I didn't understand what you said."

"Pay attention, then! You're really exactly the same, you and Erica...I always need to repeat myself. I said that I purposely wanted to be alone with you this morning and that Riccardo is a murderer."

"What?"

"Oh fine, let's go back to the beginning then. I did what I could to protect Erica from that raging lunatic, but now I absolutely need to go back to Crete. That's why I spoke so poorly of Positano, I wanted to bring all of you with me to keep the situation under control, but I need to go, I have my daughters to take care of! And I'll tell you this, too: open your eyes, don't be a sucker for appearances, they'll cause you as much trouble as they have for me; it's another reason why I decided to talk to you. I know how much you care about Erica, and I feel guilty. I'll be frank: at times, over the years, I had the feeling that you loved her more than I did...but having children, Goliarda, hardens you toward others. It's anything but enriching! As soon as you have children, everyone else becomes less precious— dispensable, that's it! It's awful, I know, but only they, your children, end up counting while you watch them grow up."

"But what's going on?" I hear myself ask, stunned by the situational U-turn and by Olivia's tears, her body trembling through her gasps and sobs. She has gotten dressed in the meantime, and, with her foulard pressed against her mouth, she is trying to hold back the emotion that has exploded inside of her, and which sounds so sinister in the middle of that blue stillness of sky and sea.

"What's going on?" she practically yells. "If I knew, I wouldn't be here torturing myself endlessly. That's what has to be found out. Erica will never admit it, especially to me; but believe me, she's not okay, she's wasting away. More than once I've heard her crying at night. That's another reason I thought of you, maybe you could get her to talk. Once she told me that she had confessed things to you that she could never say to another human soul—I remember because I was extremely jealous then, but now it's not a question of jealousy. Another sign of the seriousness of the situation was that she wanted to come here without telling you. Imagine, she was doing so badly that she didn't want you to notice, but I knew that her not wanting you here was terrible for her, and I convinced her to send you that post-card from the Fascist era—you know that I collect old post-cards. I had her write it, practically dictating the words, and I mailed it myself. I'm sure that if I hadn't, she would have torn it up."

23

In that violent fit, Olivia let out her apprehension, her fear for her sister, and even her own feelings of guilt for not being up to the task of helping her—or for not *wanting* to help her, having only ever benefited from Erica's self-sacrifice. She then left seemingly relieved of a great weight. And for the first time, as she gave me a kiss goodbye, she whispered with her beautiful, full lips: "I trust you. Thank you." But that very "thank you" made it clear that Olivia had once again unloaded her duties and responsibilities onto someone else. Looking unburdened in a weightless dress—like hordes of butterfly wings sewn together—she is heading back to her full life, the oblivious and carnal life of a fantastic animal: half tiger and, in fact, half butterfly,

I think while admiring the leap with which she hops from Lucibello's boat onto the ramp of the ship.

"She's the exact portrait of our mother—right, Riccardo?" Erica comments. "The same lightness in her movements, and the same joy in being alive..."

"I'm not sure," he replies, pensively, "sometimes she reminds me of her, and sometimes..."

"Oh, a modern version, of course. As a painter, you should spot similarities, even when done by different brushstrokes. Mom was clearly a Boldini, Olivia a Modigliani, or some Divisionist painter, something like that. Wouldn't you like to do her portrait?"

"I'm only interested in landscapes for now."

"Oh, my dear Goliarda, in the end we'll no longer have anything to remember the faces that accompanied us in life. Don't get mad, Riccardo, but for a little while now, all of the Pollocks, Mondrians, and the like, it's not that I don't like them anymore, but they frighten me. I feel like they want to erase a person's physical side, to kill it, as if to show that on earth, after a certain point... neither man nor woman exists."

"Why? Have there been any real-life humans walking around for the last thirty or so years?"

"I think so, yes, and I think I'll focus on welcoming into my collection the reviled portraitists of the early twentieth century. I was offered—at a great price—a Segantini, it's so beautiful I could go crazy. I'll buy it this very evening."

As soon as the topic of painting comes up, Riccardo moves away from us. It's clear that Olivia and painting have the power to cause disagreements between them. It's always been that way, I think, cautioning myself not to take Olivia's outburst as gospel. But the curtain of doubt that her words have stretched between me and the couple now acts on its own. That's the great power of accusations, of slander. Whoever listens loses all peace of mind and stops thinking clearly.

So, worried despite my better judgment, I started to observe them like a spy—already a horrible position for any allegedly civilized person to find herself in. And not finding any evidence of drama in their relationship, I chose not to condemn Riccardo unless I saw real proof. But as the days passed, I slowly slid into a subtle panic of doubts and fears. One side of my nature urged me to take the bull by the horns, to say everything to Erica, and thereby break the silence. Or was it better to continue to watch them, waiting passively for things to happen, events I could use as revelatory elements in the chemistry of relationships?

Erica knew me, understood me too deeply at that point not to sense that something had changed inside of me. Pushed by her own generous nature, which was never missing in action (she helped me so many times, morally and financially), she came out and said it: "Is something bothering you, Goliarda? Forgive me, but I can't stand you the way you are now. Tell me what's wrong. If, like the last time, you need money and you're not telling me . . . I'll give you a good spanking, as Fiore used to give me if I 'poisoned our peace' by withholding something from the two of them. I'll say it to you plainly, in her words: you are poisoning all the joy of seeing you again, as well as the beautiful sun out there which I'd been missing for so long."

Related in this way, her words might seem overly harsh. But I'm incapable of conveying that warm mix of seriousness and irony that from her voice to her eyes tied these sentences and their meaning in a single friendly note. Friendliness calls for friendliness, sincerity calls for sincerity, and I couldn't help but reply in the same tone, "My dear Erica, you're the one who's poisoning our relationship and this sun by withholding things."

A silent, somber calm before the storm covers Erica's thoughts and limbs, enveloping every remote corner of the living room. Not a whiff of air moves the shut curtains behind her, nor the wide sleeves that went swishing along with her voice before. The calm lingers on the low glass table separating us, lighting with a cruel glow the crystals, the pewter, the soft cloud of large bushy mimosas. Seeing as she won't talk, my tone changes again.

"Enough, Erica, I'm disappointed in you! I didn't expect that you could possibly lie, or stay silent with a friend from whom you of all people demanded complete sincerity until just yesterday. I never believed that the complete sincerity you valued so much could ever exist between two people. Now speak, or I swear you'll never see me again!"

There is enough violence in my voice to send the whole room trembling, and for a moment the glass table seems to quake sinisterly. I stand up, determined to leave and get away from this static chaos where my friend is keeping me, implacable in her silence.

I haven't gotten to the door when Erica's calm voice stops me: "My silence is only due to the fact that I'm afraid of implicating another person. I can be completely sincere, but only if that sincerity does not jeopardize the reputation of someone who's put their trust in me."

"If you want to keep quiet to protect Riccardo, I'm willing to give my consent for our former pact to be broken. But in order to do this, you and Olivia need to relieve me of all ethical responsibility over any future harm that could come to pass, for either of you."

"You talk like a lawyer," Erica now laughs, sincerely, and this laugh, so new, nearly hysterical, convinces me to come back and sit down. Not where I was seated before, but on the couch next to her.

"I am a lawyer's daughter, you know."

"Yes, and that's why, with you, I was able to free myself from the silence to which all murderers are sentenced after their crime. Now I get it—it's because of that curious inheritance that you received from your father along with your eye color. You lawyers are like priests, confessors . . ."

"That I'm a priest is no news to me. My father, who like many poor children was taught by the Jesuits, also said that when the death of the Christian God spread to the masses, the functions of the lawyer and the judge would blend more and more with the role of the ministry, the sacred . . . because, he claimed, man can't live without practicing confession."

"How beautiful you are when you talk about your father, Goliarda. You wouldn't think that you hated him all that much when he was alive."

"Unfortunately, in order to grow up, it seems you also need to hate the ones you love. But let's leave that alone. You're good at derailing the topic, you're a half lawyer yourself, Signora Erica! You're the one we were talking about."

"You're the only person who was there for me back then, and I owe it to Giacomino. Life is incredible: an unrelated person—at least in terms of family—who points out another unrelated stranger to you. Do you know, I didn't find you all that likable, with that frenzied, suffragette's air of yours. But I have to say, perhaps you atheists aren't completely wrong when you point to friendship as a possible way of finding meaning . . . You all don't get lost searching for something absolute. How you used to frighten me when you'd say that the only certainty can be found in doubt, in the acceptance of difference, and even in that troublesome yet natural side of us that we Christians call evil."

"Olivia was right, Erica, you are not yourself. And if you'll let me, I'll stay by your side and I won't ask you anything else . . . We've been here for hours, and I think that we should go look for Riccardo. You said that he went to see Pierpaolo in Praiano? We could meet him there, and see the new house they're building."

"I don't feel like it. Olivia is right, Positano has changed, it's dragging toward the end. The thing that struck me the most is that all of the old people are making a break for it: Rudy to Santagata—so far away!—Pierpaolo to Praiano,

Lietta and Lorenzo with their house always empty...it looks bricked up. Go look for Riccardo, you said? There's no point, I'd told you another lie. For two years now, even at a distance, I've told you tons of lies. I didn't want to mix you up in my feelings of disillusionment about everything."

"Was it Riccardo who drove you to feel so disillusioned, Erica?"

The sun has gone down, and, as much as I peer at the shadows filling the opposite end of the large couch, my eyes can no longer make out my friend's features. In those tormenting shadows, my fear transforms into true terror when Erica screams: "Don't judge Riccardo! He hasn't done anything wrong. Can't we give it a rest, always pointing fingers at others?"

Erica has jumped to her feet, rapid and feline; in the dark I can follow her white gown as it darts in front of me. A few leaps and all of the lights turn on in that formerly enchanted room, where even in the worst of times the two friends could once find refuge.

"Olivia too with her accusations: 'Riccardo is torturing you!' She's even claimed that he's an opportunist and is with me for money. She even brought America into it, saying that after all those years in that commercial country, he also learned the lesson. But it's not true. If you all want to know, I'm the one to blame, or it's my nature, so full of talents—as everyone tells me—but never leading me to cultivate a single one of them. Since I was a girl, I would decide to sing and I could do it, dance and I could, play tennis and I could. I'd fall in love with some painter while wandering through galleries and I could copy him—oh, perfectly!—but only copies ever came from my hands. And besides, everybody knows that talent in everything means talent in nothing. I couldn't even succeed in being a real murderer."

Distressed by her cry and by the merciless light, I have stood up and started to follow Erica as she paces from one side of the room to the other. Only when I take her in my arms do I manage to make her sit back down next to me, albeit in a strange pose, as if rejecting my hug. Her whole body has morphed into a hard bundle of nerves, a stark change that makes her face and eyes appear almost ugly. The tension, the ugliness is so unbearable that I instinctively gaze into the void as I hold her in my arms, but after a few seconds Erica's limbs finally yield like heavy, unloosed sticks against my body. She's so heavy I have to let her slide down on the couch. After languishing there for a few seconds, Erica unexpectedly begins to speak again, with even some hints of her old irony.

"Oh yes, I couldn't make it to a professional level as a murderer either. I'm nothing but a dilettante in everything, even in being a woman. What is a woman who isn't able to bring life into the world? Yes, taking out that great professional criminal named Leopoldo was nothing more than a simple act, practically handed to me by circumstances, and so nauseatingly feminine too. I didn't even have to go to the trouble of obtaining the poison, because he, the true professional, had given it to me. I almost admire him. He even managed to die the way he'd wanted. And he also had the strength to keep quiet for years. Oh, keeping quiet with strangers and acquaintances is an easy game, but with the ones we love...And Leopoldo loved me. You see, Goliarda, I discovered that the first thing one needs to learn when deciding to kill is how to keep quiet, and I mean with everyone. Do you understand the horror? All one's life keeping a secret like that? No one can hold out for too long from telling the person they love about such a terrible experience—it's the same with an exciting one—something lived fully, an inescapable part of the self. That's ultimately what drives so many people to talk about it with the first person they run into, even if it's a police-man. It's not remorse, it's the need to talk to others about a part of themselves. That's one reason why a murder com-mitted in a group—say, in the army or in a gang—is easier. Others know, they saw, they understand you to your core. No, it's impossible not to feel that you need to be truly un-derstood by the person you love, you can't turn down the happiness of giving yourself to another. I know how much it cost me not to reveal my true self to Olivia. And so with you I had to take my slice of joy and give myself over to a friend. It was such a great relief.

"Even when I was far away, the awareness that some-one somewhere in the world knew me deep down, and still loved me in spite of it, made me feel better. It was like I still had a kind mom, who could understand and forgive. That's the most awful thing that awaits a murderer: no lon-ger having a mother, truly being an orphan, forever. After what I'd done, I should never have loved again, at least not the way I'd loved in my childhood. I think you understand what I mean."

"I've understood that you told him everything about your past because, on the contrary, you did love him."

"It's hard to speak about a great love that's ended...a love begun so long ago. Knowing Riccardo, I had sworn to myself I wouldn't tell him anything, the way I never said anything to Olivia, but he gave me no choice. It happened in Beijing, during our trip around the world, in that absurd country with its absurd history, at least to me; with its icy light that never moves from dawn to dusk. In autumn, the air is so still that the dead leaves can't even fall from the trees, but hang on the branches until they dry up, a terrible sight, stiff like embalmed corpses. Riccardo was enchanted by that inhuman nature. Even the kindness of all of those little men is cold, always the same. At times you get the impression that their exquisite smiles and manners could at any moment shift into cruelty—unyielding and unrepentant, as precise and relentless as their smiles.

"From a discussion on painting we started to talk about Leopoldo; or rather, I made the mistake of referencing how much Leopoldo had told me, and how correct his judgments had been, about those countries—he had traveled all over for business. And then something I had not expected happened...Ah, Riccardo's ability not to reveal things about himself knows no bounds: sometimes I think, joking of course, that he has the real makings of a murderer...Anyway, it came to light that—oh, he didn't throw a fit about it, if only he had!—it came to light that he was jealous of Leopoldo. All night he kept me awake with questions, deductions, hypotheses. At a certain point, he said that he was sure that I still loved my uncle, and, through my uncle, Leopoldo too. He even threatened to leave me. At that point I couldn't take it anymore, and to prove to him how wrong he was, I told him everything. Right then and there he seemed relieved, and I remember he wanted to make love. Riccardo is strange, so frigid on the outside, yet so passionate in love: focused and wild . . . I hadn't known this side of him earlier."

"And did this passionate side bother you?"

"Oh no! Actually, it's what makes me feel connected to him. I'm the same way. Forgive these details, but now that I've decided to talk about it, I need to tell you everything, don't I?"

"Absolutely."

"And after that amorous dawn—it was the last one, Goliarda—he came out and said that the boldness that I'd reveal when we made love had always frightened him a bit, and now he finally understood why. It was so difficult for me to comprehend what had happened to him deep down, and now I have the same difficulty in explaining it to you. In my very sensuality he could glimpse the trace, the seed of a murderer—the inclination to kill that he had always felt was latent in all women, his mother included. It was like he had lost his mind. He had me another time, but it was awful, without any tenderness, a rape. As if he wanted to turn me into nothing. I knew that it was all over, but I didn't want to accept it, and I kept quiet, waiting, continuing to follow him through parks and museums.

"Everything had ended under that revelatory sky, in that operating-room light which leaves nothing in shadow; where every detail in faces, trees, stones is always brought inescapably into plain view. One day, however, he broke his silence and told me about a recurring dream that had haunted him since childhood: a woman was spying on him from behind the door, then she'd secretly enter his room, and, without looking at him, start to rummage through his drawers. Then, finally, he'd have sexual relations with her, but her vagina would turn into something mechanical with sharp teeth, mangling his genitals. He told me all of this in passing, almost like it was something funny, though he did say that that very dream had forced him when he was in America to undergo analysis, which lasted... but what does it matter how long it lasted! For years.

"Finally that trip came to an end, and I still hoped that in returning to our lives in our own country everything would work itself out. One night, coming back from the preview of his first exhibition, just as we were going to bed (we still slept in the large double bed together, as he preferred: 'We'll sleep together like our ancestors and not in those silly separate rooms like Americans'), he told me that the anguish that had started tearing up his insides upon learning about my crime had gotten so bad that he thought it would be for the best if we slept separately; and that perhaps the only way to heal this wound was for me to confess to the authorities, to turn myself in essentially, and that after that—yes, after—no matter the punishment the justice of men would sentence me to, he would wait for me.

"Maybe I made a mistake, but I was so bewildered, I found myself practically yelling, 'But I don't feel one bit guilty!' And I also said, 'We'll lose all the money.' I can't tell you what triggered these words. He jumped out of the bed, shouting that I was nothing but a greedy murderer, like all women—that he didn't want my money... Please, don't make me say any more, I can't take it."

Erica starts to cry, but in such a strange way it gives me chills. Motionless, I listen to sobs and moans that sound like they are coming from an infant denied its mother's breast, and I observe my friend's body regress into a small thing, curled into itself, her hands groping as if trying to clutch onto something.

It's not what my mind wants, but I find myself grabbing those little frightened hands, and I say in a joking tone of voice: "Oh, there there, little girl, sleep now. Nothing's wrong, you'll see, everything will pass with a cup of warm milk and a good night's rest, and then we'll go out on the boat, the two of us, together."

"Oh yes, Iuzza, I'm so cold and tired. Would you bring me some cookies with the milk? I didn't have a single bite to eat today."

Roused by that request expressed with a childish voice and a big, sweet smile—the same smile Erica must have had as a little girl—I run to the kitchen, where I throw together milk, bread, cookies, butter, honey, everything that I can dig up in my anxiousness. When I come back, another unexpected spectacle is waiting for me. Erica has bounced back, her hair is again neat, her gown tidied along her graceful body, her hands lying in her lap. She waits, looking serious—a pensive seriousness that's typical of children.

"How wonderful, I could eat a horse! But you'll eat too, won't you?"

I realize that, in gathering what was needed to make a meal, I've prepared for two. When did it happen? And what does it matter? What matters is witnessing the joy, the famished greediness with which she has dived into the food. And, so as not to disturb the peaceful atmosphere, I also eat, even if I'm not hungry.

Having finished eating, Erica finally looks at me and declares: "Now I'm going to sleep a bit, but you won't go, will you? You'll sleep here? After all, just this evening Riccardo went to sleep at Palazzo Murat. I think he despises this house. I was a little upset, partly because of the town. It's not that I care all that much about what other people think, but here people like me so much, and I don't think there was any need to rub it in everyone's faces that the two us, that we're now . . . But do you know what I say? His loss! Until now I've kept quiet for his sake. And as you've seen, it's not that they love me because they think I'm a saint. In fact, as Giacomino once told me, they almost hate saints in this town; if it weren't for the miracles . . . He knows that all wealth has its foundation in some crime. Now I'm going to sleep, and tomorrow we'll go out on our skiff like old times, looking for beaches."

Like a young know-it-all who has conscientiously recited a poem she committed to memory, Erica now falls asleep. The only thing left to do is to shift her sitting position on the couch so that she is lying down. I don't feel like leaving her though, or going to sleep—there's something in the way her mood changed that I'm not buying. But as soon as the lights are off, I feel incredibly sleepy. Perhaps it's a result of the hypnotic rhythm of her breathing, so calm and deep.

24

When I wake up, I have a moment of panic: Erica is no longer on the couch. Did I dream everything? No, the blanket I covered her with the night before has slid onto the floor, and her gown, a small white cloud in the half-light, lies in waves along the back of the couch. I don't even have time to jump down from where I'm sitting when a fresh, sunny voice commands: "Don't get up! Today it's me who'll bring you breakfast."

Erica—in pants and a pink silk blouse, a foulard on her beautiful head with the knot at the nape of her neck that only she can tie, her arms full with a large tray—enters from the doorway with that ancient stride which still stuns me, and causes me to say, "You're so beautiful, Erica—and what intuition! Today I'm the one who could eat a horse."

"I noticed yesterday, you know? You were only pretending to eat. Here you go, today we'll have an English-style breakfast. A long day at sea awaits us. Oh, don't think that I did everything myself. In fact, I only picked the flowers— pretty, aren't they? The rest is the work of Nunziatina, she came very early today. She knew that Riccardo slept elsewhere and she was worried about me. She didn't ask me anything though, that's not her style. The locals in this town do have such discreet style, Goliarda! You can find even more beautiful places, but never the kind of class these people have . . . It's a town made up mostly of artisans. I find that anyone who comes from a family of shoe cobblers, woodworkers, tailors, dyers, has an innate nobility to them—including in their hands."

Once again, we talk aimlessly of our favorite topics, while we spread butter and jam on the toast, she sipping tea, I coffee. No one entering that bright room could possibly imagine the whirlwind of emotions that passed between us only a few hours earlier.

I see it in Riccardo's expression when he stands in the doorway, unsure whether to enter or to turn around. His hesitancy only lasts a few seconds, but I'm already on high alert about this presence in Erica's life and so I pick up on it, and I also notice a certain degree of disappointment, even if he tries to hide it with the deliberately joyful—too joyful—movement with which he springs in our direction.

"Here they are, my two magnificent goddesses at court. I swear, you're both splendid! Careful not to evoke the wrath of Olympus. By Jove, if I were Juno, I would be crazy with jealousy over you two."

Even this joke rings false, and isn't nearly as witty as he'd like. Without holding back, I decide to stare at that face, which is perfect even with the creases that time has begun to add with the most refined artistry. Under that perfection, even his cold sky-blue eyes, after their initial surprise, have recomposed themselves in bright and broad glances; but his halting gestures are too rigid, if not awkward. What was he expecting to find coming here so early after a night—perhaps the first—spent apart? It's impossible to say, but what is clear to me is his disappointment, and the very words he's now uttering are only further confirmation.

"I see that my absence agrees with you, Erica...You're not going to give me a kiss? Or were you unwell, and so Goliarda stayed and slept over? I knew it, dear, and frankly, if there's one thing I envy you for it's Goliarda's friendship. Every time that I've been unwell, I haven't found a dog willing to stay by my side."

This last remark provokes a blind feeling of irritation in me.

"You probably never really looked for a dog."

What I've said causes an uncomfortable silence, and I almost want to run out of the room. But I have to stay. Even if I didn't have a promise to keep, my entire relationship with Riccardo has been put into question now, and I need to figure out who this person I thought I knew really is, and what he wants from the two of us.

Riccardo, likely sensing that I won't abandon Erica, decides to break the silence. His voice changes again, and I think of how many times I felt moved by that same warm and tender voice.

"I'm afraid that you're right, Goliarda, each of us gets what they deserve. Yes, I admit it, I don't know how to ask, and I suffer the consequences."

Now his face, along with his voice, expresses such intense suffering—his eyes have turned a dark blue with traces of red, the red of held-back tears—that he almost makes me reverse my decision, pushing me toward my old trust in him. But the calm beach of trust has been flooded by waves of doubt, and, more than sympathy or affection, I simply feel defeated, powerless, the way we always do when we would or should help someone else but can't.

I've stood up while thinking this, and I tell him ruefully, "I feel bad for you, Riccardo, but I can't help. No one can help anyone."

As if in response to my remark, that faint, once again childish voice—the young Erica I met for the first time last night—exclaims: "Oh, wait, Goliarda, wait. I'll come with you. The boat should be ready, and the sun is gorgeous outside."

A small, trembling hand grabs mine. I find myself squeezing it tightly, without looking again at Erica or Riccardo.

We're already on the stairs when he shouts cheerfully: "Have a good swim! What a great idea, just like old times. I'll stay here for an hour or so to paint, and then I'll come join you. See you soon, girls...You're both splendid. I think that even when you're seventy, you'll still be two young lassies bursting with joie de vivre."

Outside the house, Erica's hand stops trembling in mine, and now she's the one squeezing and pulling me along.

"I feel that Riccardo is right. What would you say if our lives came to an end here together, in our Shangri-la—decrepit, but surrounded by friends to help us, and in front of us this sea we love so much?"

"Oh, it doesn't sound half bad. And we already have Irma and Edna to look to as an example. You know that they still go swimming nearly year-round? And to think they look like paraplegics when they're in town; then on the beach they dive fearlessly into the water, no matter the weather, like Olympic champions...There's also that old sculptor with his sister...I saw him yesterday...he's getting more handsome every year in his old age. Now he looks just like a snow-covered tree..."

"Wait, you didn't even get to wash up. Should we turn back?"

"No way! I'll take a bath later."

"But you might be uncomfortable."

"Not at all, one of the nicest things about the movies is you get used to jumping from your bed straight to the set, without worrying about brushing your teeth or anything. It reminds you of leaving the house for school still feeling warm from your sheets. Once I noticed that an assistant director had pajamas on under his pants, and when I pointed it out to him, he replied, 'Oh, I haven't done this since high school. It's sweet'—those were his very words—'a sweet necessity.' Maybe it's another reason why people in showbiz never get old."

"You miss doing that work, don't you, Goliarda?"

"Oh, I do, but I'll drown my feelings in a nice peach granita. It's so hot today, or is it because I'm dirty? I have a friend who claims that washing is bad for you, that it's an unhealthy American trend; the filth protects from the elements. Actually, you met him! It's Gigi Vanzi, yes, the one who hates going into the sea."

"But he doesn't seem dirty."

"Exactly, he claims that the more we bathe, the dirtier we get."

Erica laughs as she walks into Giacomino's café. Her laugh immediately surprises the pastry chef, who is clearly "in the know" about everything, and was concerned for his princess. But what does he know, exactly? I need to talk to him later, I tell myself as I gobble down two peach granitas; even if it goes against the rules of the town's game, an exception can be made for once.

"Oh no, Goliarda, I don't mind you asking me, partly because I know you're as silent as the grave. Unfortunately, I can't tell you anything specific, only impressions—and can we trust our impressions? There's only one thing that I can define as more than just a feeling, and it's the fact that I—through ways that would be too complicated to explain: it's a small world, and as you know, we often go to Milan and to New York—anyway, I know for sure that the youngster still sees his first wife, and that not only does she appear to be incredibly beautiful—so they've told me—but by all accounts she's a quick one, maybe too quick. You know how Olivia is, she doesn't know how to keep her mouth shut... She didn't tell you? That's odd, but the last time she was here she really was out of sorts, poor thing! Now tell me: this morning, after he spent the night out, how did everything go?"

"Oh, perfectly fine, seemed like nothing had happened... Did you know that today we're going to Capri? There's a big party tonight. He'll be coming, too."

25

The trip to Capri, the party at one of the
many villas perched on the rocks, the ride back
on Erica's friend's forty-foot-long boat which
cut through the calm sea with its powerful
sails, the dolphins that leaped jubilantly in the
sun like unsheathed scimitars: all of it helped
to ease my worries. That fight was probably
just the classic, slightly sadomasochistic game
played by all couples who are bound with such
assured passion that they give splitting up a try
just to feel again the freshness of when they first
met, now that their relationship has fallen prey
to monotony. Even constant happiness becomes
tiresome, and a fight or a temporary break can
be an antidote to habit, which is humanity's true

curse, forever threatening the joys of love, of work, or of friendship.

That must be it, I tell myself again as I close my bags. The time for my vacation has run out, and, with something resembling joy running through my limbs and my relaxed mind, I get ready to face my other life in Rome, which only a month ago seemed like hell to me. Maybe for Erica and Riccardo that fight was nothing but a vacation of pain after years of happiness. For me too, I think, it would be impossible to stay here forever in this peacefulness; it would only be lost in the end, whereas going back to the real world will allow me to find it once again upon my return, just as it was before.

In those final days of reestablished peace in our threesome, when Riccardo would look at me, I sometimes thought I could glimpse in his probing eyes the strain of waiting, of suspicion. Considering his extreme modesty, I finally justified it as a plausible reaction to the thought that Erica had told me about their disagreement during that nightmare of an evening. Nothing could be more natural, given that for years they had perfectly maintained their commitment to not involving anyone else in private matters: a fact, incidentally, that had always made them so agreeable to their mutual friends. Only once, Lorenzo, who was always such a critic of behaviors and personalities, exclaimed: "They could at least disagree about how they take their tea! Probably, friends, we are witnessing a relationship between gods who are perfect in body and soul..."

And Erica? I ask myself, thinking back over the last few days—so close, yet already distant in light of my imminent departure. It's always that way when preparing to leave a place: the body might be just outside, waiting for the taxi, but the mind can already filter everything through the truthful lens of "after." Erica was, as always, at times distant, at times too pale underneath her light tan which never becomes a thick coating. I hear her words again: "Maybe, Goliarda, the right thing to do would be to go to the police and confess everything. I'd get rid of this wealth which has become a burden, just as it has for Riccardo. But would they believe me? Or would they take me for a crazy woman?" She gave a long laugh as she went on: "That would really take the cake—instead of a wholesome prison, ending up in an insane asylum."

I was immediately startled at the time, but her facetious look and her childlike laughter dispelled the feeling before it could sink in; and as hard as I tried to rewatch that moment objectively—waiting under the hot sun for a taxi that, as usual, was late—I couldn't see any reason to worry about her mental state. So then why was that oppressive feeling nagging at me? Was it the unnaturally strong October sun, or the taxi that just wouldn't arrive? It's hunger, I decide—it might mean missing the taxi, but I need to put something into my stomach, and Giacomino's is right around the corner anyway. I said goodbye to him yesterday, but he won't be shocked to see me again. It's inevitable in Positano: the more you say goodbye to people—the more you solemnly announce your departure—the harder it becomes to leave.

Entering the café, I remind myself not to get trapped in unending farewells, but to sneak away as I always have in the past, so that the commanding spirit of Positano might not notice I'm fleeing. It has the power, that spirit, to stop you as soon as it knows you intend to leave.

But the pastry chef seems so surprised when he looks at me from behind the counter that despite myself, I ask, "What's wrong, Giacomino?"

"What's wrong is that the youngster spent all night at the Buca di Bacco playing poker. I found out from Filiberto an hour ago—he was thrilled because he had won a ton of money off him. I didn't know he had a gambling habit too, but that's not what worries me. It's that after, at dawn, he took off in a taxi."

A wave of apprehension, of guilt—how to describe the feeling?—sends me flying out of the café, without even thinking about my suitcases or—and this might give an idea of my level of distress—the briefcase with the first draft of my book. I run so fast that at a certain point I feel like all of those steps leading up to the sky have turned into an avalanche of white boulders rolling toward me.

Only when I hear my fist knock against the wooden front door—which is as familiar to me now as the one to my childhood home—do I stop, shaking from exhaustion, and from a new sensation, perhaps more terrible than my earlier distress: the white lacquered door gives way without resistance, opening wide. Why am I so frightened by that silence? Is it not one of the unique features of Erica's house, one that has always made me remember my time spent there with her like a now-lost golden age of my own life?

In the dimly lit living room, I remember that it's Sunday, a day off for Nunziata and the others. In fact, on weekdays, at that hour, all the doors and windows are thrown open for southern-style cleaning—pillows, blankets, sheets, everything waiting outside to be shaken in the fresh air. I'm about to head toward the bedroom when I pick up an imperceptible smell of croissants or cakes: did she, that masterful baker, get up early to make something for her friends? A Nordic cake, something simple with a mild taste: "Just to have a change from all those mountains of sugar and aromas, which are the norm in our country, the first point of contact with the East," I heard her say the first Sunday I stayed with her, surprised to find her already awake, cheerfully busying herself in the kitchen.

A faint clanging of crockery directs me to the kitchen. Instead of Erica, I find Nunziatina. Hearing me enter, she spins around and stares at me, mute and stiff like a puppet on a well-oiled hinge.

"Oh, it's you, Signorina! Excuse me, but I got scared, I thought you'd left. Would you like a coffee? I brought croissants, my mistress loves them."

"Thank you, Nunziata, gladly. I'm starving to death. Is Erica still sleeping?"

"She wasn't here when I arrived, and the bed was made, but I didn't think anything of it—my mistress always makes her bed before leaving on Sundays . . . She says they had to make it every day at her house, you know? They're raised so properly, those gentlemen and ladies in the north . . . It has always amazed me."

"But why exactly are you here?"

"Ah, early today I heard that the young man had gone in a taxi, and, well, I was worried! No, no, finish your coffee . . . When I saw that she wasn't in, I sent Tonino, Giacomino's nephew, down to the marina to ask Teresa if she had already gone out to sea. That was only twenty minutes ago: even for a child it would take at least—Oh, here he is though, do you hear how he's running?"

Tonino, red in the face and agitated, sits down in the first chair that he finds and says, "Nobody's seen her at the docks. I asked everyone, even the priest. Lucibello told me to ask him. Said that sometimes she goes to church on Sunday."

"But where could she be?" Nunziata practically shouts, slipping off the hinge that had been holding her while she brings her nervous hands to her chest. Suddenly I remember the bizarre bunker hidden in the bowels of the house, which Erica called her refuge. Only once did she show it to me.

"The bunker!" I yell, jumping to my feet.

"What did you say, Signorina?" Nunziata's bewildered voice echoes back at me.

"You know, that room downstairs where the well was. Erica told me that only you knew about it, so you could clean it."

"Oh my, how did I not think of it! You're right, she could be down there working."

I'm again gripped by fear as I walk down all of those stairs behind that barefoot woman who's scurrying like a monkey along the countless, steep, spiraling stairs, down and down through the building's walls. My heeled shoes are made for the city...In fact, I'd already left, I tell myself as I take them off, cursing for once that town which is nothing but stairs, both indoors and out.

When I catch up to her, she has already opened the trapdoor, disappearing through it. I'm only halfway down the stairs when a scream stops me. I have to sit down or I'll slip under that crushing wave, that voice as it shouts: "Oh God, I knew it! My poor mistress, I knew it!"

I knew it too, the tremor running through my whole body tells me, while my curiously empty head passively accepts without the slightest shock what I had been expecting for some time.

I could stay there forever, now that my entire body has turned into a heavy, unfeeling block of ice, when a deep, all-consuming silence insidiously takes the place of the scream from a moment before. That silence warns my frozen mind: watch out for Nunziata! She's pregnant. She could have fainted or hurt herself down there where you, a coward, do not even want to look.

My senses wake up from their feverish sleep—I even feel drenched in sweat—and send me flying down into the night that is still reigning below. It's completely dark, besides the halo of a lamp that's hanging from a lofty birch branch, shedding a pinkish glow on the back of an armchair. A small figure sits there, composed like a wax sculpture, and Nunziata kneels before it, hands clenched, face ashen, staring with such a fanatical expression it could make the soul shiver with fear.

Paralyzed from surprise as much as grief, I can only behold that funereal arrangement, which is so ancient I feel myself diving into an entire past full of mysteries, sacrifices, rituals, sedimented in the caverns of my contemplative mind.

I wouldn't dare disturb that scene, if it weren't for Nunziata breaking the silence with the gentlest of voices: "She smells like a rose. Come, smell her."

I now realize that the smell, which I had attributed to some bouquet of flowers placed in a dark corner of the room, is coming from her. My eyes have adjusted to the dark, and before approaching Nunziata I take a good look around: there are no flowers, no sweets, which sometimes indoors can give off a floral smell. As soon as Nunziata feels my presence near her, she looks at me, and, with eyes dilated as though possessed by a mystic vision, she signals to kneel down next to her. I know that bringing her back to reality could harm her much more than her current sleepwalking state, and so I am forced to look at every detail of what I strangely feel is a personal defeat; as if my friend's suicide were nothing but a warning, the continually feared and denied revelation of my own fate.

That's why I am so cold, I tell myself, observing that delicate face that's only slightly paler than usual, that body which has perhaps turned stiff under the soft waves of silk, although—elegant and foresighted up to the end—she has succeeded in hiding this stiffness by wearing the gown I've known for so long. Her hands are not tense, and what strikes me the most when I look at her face is that her eyes are not wide open or glassy, but almost half closed by her long, full, hay-colored lashes.

"She's smiling!" Nunziata exclaims once more. "She's smiling and smells of flowers... Oh, look, the ring she always wore, it fell on the ground."

"Don't touch it!" I rush to say, realizing that Nunziata is coming back to her senses. "We mustn't touch a thing—for the police, you understand."

At the police station, we end up in what's less an interrogation than a family reunion—it could be any family struck by sudden loss like lightning out of clear skies. Expressions of dismay, words of kindness for Nunziata who's lost someone dear to her, heartfelt understanding for the great sorrow they imagine I'm experiencing.

The general warmth of these men in uniform—which is so incongruous in those two bare rooms—unties the knots of self-imposed dignity that have been binding me, and I break out in tears. I cry for so long I become dizzy, like a traveler through the freezing cold who is given a cup of red wine to drink. Though this cup doesn't contain alcohol, but coffee. It's not my imagination—those big, soldierly, clean-shaven men have had coffee, cappuccinos, and croissants brought over from the nearby café. In a corner, the captain sits at his desk, dunking croissants in his steaming cup of hot milk as if he were at home.

While I've been crying, the two rooms have filled up with people who knew Erica; some were called on, others have arrived of their own accord. A true funeral vigil, I think, and I feel joyous gratitude toward all of those people whom Erica loved, and whom she was right to love.

Tears well up again and fall more softly now that Giacomino's strong and tender hand—a hand that knows how to wield the spade, but also to delicately engrave a tree trunk—has rested on my shoulder.

After a long and discreet pause, he speaks to me.

"I brought your bags and your briefcase . . . I imagine you'll leave in the afternoon."

"Yes," I reply, almost with terror, returning to the reality of the work that's waiting for me in Rome. "Thank you, it's a good thing the briefcase wasn't lost."

I'm expecting something pragmatic from Giacomino—for hours now I've been hearing comments like *Such a beautiful and happy woman* and *What was she ever lacking in life?*—and so when he begins to talk again, I'm left stunned by his hard, brisk tone.

"Listen, Goliarda, you were closer to her than I was. You don't think we could nail the youngster for this?"

He's struck so directly at the heart of my own desire to know how much Riccardo did or didn't want Erica to die, that I hear the desperation in my words: "If there was a crime, Giacomino, there's no way to prove it. A white crime, my father would say, one that eludes men, and the law. Maybe it would have been possible to show that he used insidious weapons, psychological ones, to gain control of Erica's estate and push her to suicide."

"Why 'would have'?"

"Because Erica left a letter in which she asks for everyone's forgiveness for what she's done; in which she thanks Olivia, her nieces, but especially her husband, Riccardo, for these last years of joy, and for having been her ally—that's exactly what she wrote—in fighting the idea of suicide that had haunted her."

Giacomino has become so quiet next to me that I have to look at him. Who knows why I didn't do so before: he's as pale as a ghost, with yellowish splotches of rage on his forehead, splotches of powerlessness, I think. And while I wait for him to rebel in some way, I see his whole face recompose itself into its usual calm. His honey-colored eyes reveal a sadness that he's never shown me before, as if all of the sorrows and injustices of man were parading by in front of his eyes. I don't dare say a word, overpowered, too, by that vision, and I'd expect anything in the world from him, anything except for him saying, "Women!"

· 26 ·

I didn't return to Positano for a long time, nor did I hear any news about Olivia or Riccardo. I wasn't interested; our almost-friendship hadn't been anything more than a reflection of Erica. What had happened to her was like a warning, and I too tried with all of my might to fight the dark pull of suicide which for a decade swept away so many of our generation. Not all of them resorted to poison, many let themselves die of inaction. It might have had to do with the winds of complete and utter change that swept through our country.

Only after I also had dared to cast a glance into the black hole of nonbeing—though unable, in the end, to let myself fall, held back perhaps by a disproportionate sense of curiosity which has always been the cornerstone of my nature, or simply because there was no one there to give me a good push—I felt once again a desire to go back to that little town, a place that held intact its humanity of faces and stones, its clear sea in which to rinse our "sins," and those of others. Where I could rest the palms of my hands on the rocks and the trunks of still-whole carob trees, and pray, there where the happiness of being young had remained untouched—at least in my mind—like a butterfly kept under the immortal glass of memory.

I took the first train to Naples and then the ship. I'd firmly decided not to slip into the trap of noting how things had inevitably gone downhill. Instead I'd only try to see old friends again, and to participate in the usual "catching up," which is so essential for anyone who loves to take stock of their own life and the lives of others. How, while living, can you reach an understanding of who you were and who you've become without friends, the only witnesses—at least if you don't have children—to you and your growth?

The cement had spread, of course, and with it, an indefinable atmosphere reminiscent of a luxury clinic. But nothing ever truly dies, and everything returns. The place's true spirit, which under the impact of mass uniformity and accessibility had seemed to recoil into itself, was already beginning to make a counterattack.

The first pleasant surprise was Nicola himself, who, seemingly young again, had gone back to dreaming in his boat. Now he recalled the days when he thought only about making money as a period of youthful madness—inspired by the devil, no doubt.

"Oh, Signora Goliarda, the devil exists, all right! He takes on a different shape for every generation. For you it was Fascism, for us it's money, and, I'm afraid looking around, for these kids it will be something even more terrible... There's no question about it: drugs. The last time I was in America, five years ago, it was like a plague. And by now we know that as wonderful as that country can be, other things come from there besides Coca-Cola and all that stuff... Ah, Princess Erica! She stayed my great love... But I'm sure you remember..."

I am happy to discover that in all of these years none of the old *positanesi* have died. Lucibello is still yelling as he runs along the beach, Filiberto has gone back to studying the stars at night (now his wife takes care of everything by herself), and the tobacco shop owner just last summer celebrated his first billion lire and gave everyone gifts. Now, you tell me, where else in the world can you find someone including others in his own good fortune, and so resoundingly?

"Oh, go see Giacomino, he'll be happy to see you. Yeah, the old fox seems rejuvenated after having his daughter. You should see how he keeps her close to him! And none of the others from his generation were able to follow in his footsteps... Oh no, no one else managed to get their wife pregnant at that age. The butcher practically killed himself from all the effort."

He laughs, Nicola, and I head up the stairs toward my friend's café. Who's to say that by turning the corner into one of those little streets, I won't run into Erica, the princess. My heart is beating a bit, remembering what I've been told. It seems that sometimes she comes out of her old house and wanders through the town, light on her naked feet, even more beautiful than she was in life, and happier, too—and of course she is, because they say that she always has three little girls with her, who laugh as they run in front of her, or follow behind her calling *Mamma! Mamma!*

The beautiful princess, so good yet so unhappy, has now joined the ranks of the many myths and ghosts that populate the Amalfi Coast. An important reason is that everyone is convinced that if she had stayed in Positano forever—as she often said she'd like to do—she would not have killed herself. They have unanimously erased that little truth, convincing themselves instead that she took her life in Milan. How can you contradict them? Is it possible for one to commit suicide in Positano? Some even swear they saw her leave...

Giacomino—why overemphasize it or act surprised?—is still exactly the same. He hugs me warmly and says: "You can't, you simply can't spend so much time away from this town. It's no good for you—you're so pale. But after you go up and down our streets two or three times, taking in the sun, then you'll be back to the way you were."

With him I can finally inquire about more concrete things.

"Well, you know, it's not a lie, it's just that no one liked saying that our Erica died here. And besides, talk about it could hurt tourism...The house? It's stayed closed. Olivia came to take some things, mementos of her sister, but she

didn't reach out to me. And to tell you the truth, I was relieved. I never liked her all that much... The other guy,
the youngster? He never came back to Positano. Nunziata, who's looked after the house, she would know. Even
for Erica's paintings he found a Milanese firm to deal with
everything... Imagine not taking them with you, with the
value they must have today. The fact that he never came
back also confirmed in my eyes that there was something
shady in the whole business. In my opinion he's afraid—of
the town and of the house too. Erica's only true home, as
she always used to say, remember? Another thing—and
even if it came as no great surprise, it still pains me—was
that the guy got back together with his first wife, the American, and they even have kids... Oh sure, he still paints,
that's what Morgan says. Matter of fact, Morgan heard you
were here and told me that he'll be expecting you whenever
you like... What was I saying? Oh yeah, he still paints, and
has been more or less successful. But anyway, let's leave the
past alone, why don't you tell me about yourself instead..."

PLACES, CHARACTERS, HAPPINESS

by Angelo Pellegrino

It was Goliarda's work in film that brought her to Positano. The first time was to shoot the documentary *Festa a Positano* (Celebration in Positano) with the director Francesco Maselli, the second was to scout out locations for the feature-length film *Gli sbandati* (*Abandoned*). In the novel *Meeting in Positano*, Goliarda inverts the order of these events for narrative reasons.

It was in the first few years of the 1950s.

"Positano can cure you of anything. It opens your eyes to your past suffering and illuminates your present ones, often saving you from making further mistakes." This is what Goliarda makes the protagonist of her novel say, assigning to her an idea that had always been her own. Her faith in the powers of that seaside village on the Amalfi

Coast goes back to the years of rediscovered life after the horrors of war—a war that had kept Goliarda away from the sea for at least a decade. The nearest beaches, the ones outside Rome, remained strewn with mines for years.

Life's return in the postwar years was for Goliarda a rediscovery of the sea. It's hard to express how important it was for a person like her to be near it. One only needs to think that in Positano, even during her darkest period, which brought her close to suicide, she would still manage to find the strength to dive from a twenty-meter height. She always missed it in Rome; deep down the sea was the only thing that she never succeeded in replacing with something else after the difficult separation from her native Sicily, a separation that was only physical rather than spiritual.

Finding Positano, however, was pure serendipity, the happiness of a sudden discovery. She didn't expect it. For her it was a vital revelation, discovering this other sea which was not by an island nor hard to reach—not even that far from Rome, in the end—and yet just as beautiful as the one in Sicily despite their differences. And this revelation would bind her to that sea, at least in her thoughts, for the rest of her life. The fact that those waters washed up against a nearly hidden town like Positano, which she had known nothing about beforehand, led to a conviction that she'd found a spiritual refuge, her own Shangri-La, where all worries naturally vanished.

There are places that seem inherently happy, even if, as we all know, they aren't enough to make us happy on their own. If our spirit is in too dire a state of distress, these places will actually push us to flee from them; but if the pain isn't anything serious, they can heal us like a good balm. What's more, if our spirit is serene when this encounter takes place, or if it naturally veers on the side of serenity, the two can end up being wed in a happiness beyond all description.

Goliarda was always grateful for Rome, which even during the war years represented her own sense of freedom. But it meant a great deal to her every time she fled the city and its attendant alienation and malaise, its worldly affairs and the film industry, to take refuge in Positano, where the locals had a sweetness, an affability, a hospitality toward foreigners that already went back ages. Only those who have experienced this welcoming attitude know its priceless value. It's no coincidence that as early as the 1920s, many artists and intellectuals from around the world began to leave Capri, which had become too expensive, and went instead to Positano to find a shelter and sanitorium from the century's ills. Some never left the place again, desiring to die there, and remain, at least with their bones, in the small, florid cemetery above the town, looking out on that immense sea. Goliarda would have liked to do just that, in fact she fantasized about bringing her adored mother, Maria Giudice, to live there, taking her away from the sad town of Verano in the north.

Goliarda was a classic Sicilian from the area near Mount Etna. For her, the sea was always, and inevitably, the one depicted in Giovanni Verga's *I Malavoglia*, in *Horcynus Orca*:

the sea by Ognina, Aci Trezza, the Strait of Messina (but also by the Plaja di Catania, and the shore of lava rock under the railway). For her, the sea was Sicily. At first, she was disoriented by the discovery of another Mediterranean—and of another humanity—in Positano, Capri, Amalfi, and the whole Amalfi Coast, one that was milder and more magical, serene to the point of being schmaltzy. It was so different from the possessed sea full of cyclopean isles she'd known in Sicily, almost tragic in its drama. But toward the end of her first stay for the documentary, a new connection had been made: between her spirit, always attracted to serenity—external factors permitting—and the objective happiness that can be found in Positano. From that point on, for at least the following ten years, as soon as Goliarda could, and whenever her work allowed it, she would travel to Positano. She would even go in the winter, coming back stronger every time, and full of new ideas. The first spark for the character of Modesta in *The Art of Joy* was struck in that town.

Until an unthinkable inpouring of money made its way to that little beach. The good people of Positano became business-oriented, many gardens disappeared while cement took their place, and Positano was no longer what it once had been. Even its relationship with nonlocals changed. It was one of the effects of the economic boom that changed the face of Italy.

Inevitably, Goliarda's Positano no longer exists today. Who can bring back the smells of the missing gardens, the open spaces in the sky above the low buildings, the enchanted silences, that simple lifestyle, that way of stopping to take in the passing of time, which back then only the happy few knew how to appreciate and which seemed like primitivism to many.

It's no longer there for anyone who knew *that* Positano. But a young person encountering Positano for the first time today can still form that bond of beneficial enchantment which Goliarda experienced in the early 1950s. A place's spirit, when it has one, does not disappear easily—it withdraws and hides, but it's always there, and can still jump out suddenly when you least expect it.

Goliarda, however, as she began to go less and less frequently to Positano, only idealized the place more in her memory. When during the last part of her life she discovered the narrow streets of Gaeta—and more precisely, the seaside village of Elena where I had a house—she felt as if she had uncovered a new Positano that was closer to Rome and more accessible, so abundant were the similarities.

In Gaeta, in house number 8, Vico 4 Indipendenza, she finished writing *The Art of Joy*. And in that same little street, in 1984, she wrote in a flash the novel you've now read. In a flash because she composed it right on the heels of *L'università di Rebibbia* (The University of Rebibbia) and *Le certezze del dubbio* (The Certainties of Doubt), without ever stopping. Having once again found a publisher—namely, Rizzoli, which had decided to publish *L'università*—she worked ceaselessly, hoping that a new future had opened up for the publication of her books. She was already planning *Un amore sotto il fascismo* (Love under Fascism), a wide-ranging historical novel focusing on the figure of her mother.

Things didn't work out that way, as we know. The rejection by publishers of *Le certezze del dubbio* left her feeling stuck, and *Meeting in Positano* remained her last book.

For a long time she had wanted to write about that town on the Amalfi Coast, but Goliarda didn't like merely describing places. As in the case of San Berillo, the Catania neighborhood explored in *Io, Jean Gabin* (I, Jean Gabin), this time, too, she needed to place in her chosen setting a story and a character—places are always "acted upon" in her books, they are dynamic, never statically described. She then thought of the figure of Erica in *Meeting in Positano*, a woman who had actually been her friend, though she had a different name, and who really had died from suicide, but in Milan. It seems that only these two biographical differences separate the character from the real-life figure. Goliarda had really met "Erica," a woman from the Milanese bourgeoisie—as she told me—during the first half of the 1950s, and it seems she was, at least in part, a model for the character of Joyce in *The Art of Joy*. But Goliarda hadn't been able to fully explore the whole personality of her friend in that character; she felt the need to return to her years later, retracing how they had met and the time they had spent together in *that* Positano, about which she already wanted to write.

The real existence of the protagonist Erica, and the presence in the novel of Goliarda herself as a character, make *Meeting in Positano* a part of her *Autobiografia delle contraddizioni* (Autobiography of Contradictions), the cycle that began with *Lettera aperta* (Open Letter) in 1967. She too considered the book in this way. But there is an immense distance between this novel and that early work (it's worth remembering that in the early 1980s, Goliarda was reading a lot of Henry James). More precisely, the book relates back to her more recent approach to autobiographical writing that began with *L'università di Rebibbia*, in which the use of the autobiographical "I" changes position in the text, stepping to the side, becoming almost a backup in the telling of other people's stories. These people were more important to her than herself, but they were also an essential part of a period of her own life and, for this reason, were worth recovering and being brought to life for the reader.

It was one of the great aims of her literary art.

LIFE OF GOLIARDA SAPIENZA

· BACKGROUND ·

1880 (April 27): Birth of Maria Giudice, Goliarda's mother.

1884 (March 17): Birth of Giuseppe Sapienza, Goliarda's father.

1902–05: Maria Giudice begins to work with trade unions and in journalism. Enrollment in the Socialist Party. First arrest. Maria meets the anarchist Carlo Civardi, then takes refuge in Switzerland to avoid prison. She meets with Angelica Balabanoff, Lenin, and Mussolini.

1904–13: Maria Giudice has seven children with Carlo Civardi, with whom she is in an "open marriage": Josina (1904), Cosetta (1905), Licia (1906), Ivanoe (1909),

Danilo (1911), Olga (1913), and one other. The family lives in abject poverty and moves to Milan in 1910. Maria is fired from her work as an elementary school teacher for "immoral conduct."

1907–11: Marriage of Giuseppe Sapienza and Lucia Musumeci, and birth of their three sons: Alfio Goliardo (1907), Libero (1909), and Carlo Marx (1911). Lucia Musumeci dies in 1915, aged twenty-seven.

1911: Giuseppe Sapienza becomes secretary of the Catania local trade union.

1916: Maria Giudice becomes the first woman to hold the post of secretary at Turin's trade union. The following year she is appointed secretary to the Socialist Federation of Turin province and becomes editor-in-chief of the socialist weekly *Il grido del popolo* (The Cry of the People), which counts Antonio Gramsci among its contributors.

1917 (October 3): Carlo Civardi dies in war.

1918–20: Maria Giudice is condemned to three years' imprisonment for inciting workers at an arms factory to stop work. Freed the following year, she meets Giuseppe Sapienza at a demonstration in Tuscany and sets up house with him in Catania in 1920. They share their home with six of Maria's children (Josina, the eldest, stays in Lombardy) and Giuseppe's three children.

1920–22: In Sicily Maria campaigns for communities to manage their own land and for the introduction of a minimum wage. She and Giuseppe run the Catania union office and the newspaper *Unione*, whose premises are set on fire by the Fascists on two occasions. The Fascists also try to assassinate Maria and Giuseppe. On May 16, 1921, Goliardo, one of Giuseppe's sons, is found drowned; it is unclear whether this assassination is the work of the Mafia or the Fascists. In October of the same year Maria and Giuseppe have their first daughter, Goliarda. She dies within a few days.

· CHILDHOOD ·

1924 (May 10): Goliarda Sapienza is born in Catania.

1925–28: The family suffers devastating disruptions. Three of the children die in tragic circumstances: Josina Civardi (of pleurisy after spending a night in a rice field to escape Fascist militias), José Civardi (found hanged in prison), and Goliardo-Danilo, the youngest of the family. To make matters worse, Giuseppe Sapienza becomes infatuated with the fifteen-year-old Olga Civardi. Olga's sister Licia Civardi decides to leave Catania with her. Maria travels to Stradella with her two daughters to help them set up home. There was a precedent to this incestuous infatuation a few years earlier, between Giuseppe and another of Maria's daughters, Cosetta, when she was in her early teens.

1933: The Sapienza-Giudice family moves to Civita, a working-class neighborhood in Catania, home to craftsmen and tradesmen of every sort, and to prostitutes.

1938: Goliarda leaves school, and her mother shows the first signs of a psychological breakdown.

· EARLY YEARS IN ROME ·

1940: Goliarda starts working for a Sicilian theater company and prepares for the entrance exam for the Accademia d'arte drammatica in Rome. The following year she secures a grant to fund her course of study there. Maria Giudice moves to Rome with her.

1942: Giuseppe Sapienza is arrested and held in Catania's prison from February 2 to May 18.

1942–44: Goliarda performs onstage, often in works by Pirandello, but she stops attending her course when Italy signs an armistice with the Allies in September 1943: this marks the start of Germany's occupation of Italy and of the anti-Fascist resistance. Giuseppe

Sapienza moves to Rome and sets up the Vespri brigades. Goliarda enlists in the brigade under a false name. She is hunted down by the German police and hides in a convent. This is one of the most difficult periods in Goliarda's life; she suffers the strains of war, Nazi persecution, hunger, and a violent bout of tuberculosis. Her mother's mental health also deteriorates: Maria is hospitalized in a psychiatric asylum. Come the fall of 1944, with the war nearly over, Goliarda returns to the Accademia. But she joins student demonstrations and eventually abandons her studies.

1945–52: Goliarda devotes herself to theater. In 1945, along with Silverio Blasi and Mario Landi, she sets up the avant-garde theater company T45, then in 1946 she joins the Compagnia del piccolo teatro d'arte. In 1948 she meets the future film director Francesco (Citto) Maselli, marking the start of an eighteen-year relationship. In 1950 she and Silverio Blasi set up the Compagnia del teatrino Pirandello. The following year she receives great acclaim for her role in Pirandello's *Vestire gli ignudi*.

1949 (November 24): Giuseppe Sapienza dies in Palermo.

1953 (February 5): Maria Giudice dies in Rome from complications due to bronchitis. Her wake is attended by Umberto Terracini, the former president of the Constituent Assembly, and Sandro Pertini and Giuseppe Saragat, both future presidents of the Italian republic.

1953–55: Goliarda and Citto entertain many intellectual and filmmaker friends. Goliarda becomes friends with Luchino Visconti, who casts her in *Medea* at the Manzoni Theater in Milan, and then, in 1954, in the film *Senso*. Goliarda meets Haya Harareet, and they become close friends.

1956: Revelations of Stalin's crimes bring on an ideological crisis. Goliarda has increasingly frequent anxiety attacks. She starts to write poetry (later to be published in the anthology *Ancestrale*).

1957: Goliarda works as an assistant on Visconti's film *Le notti bianche* (*White Nights*).

· WRITING ·

1958: Goliarda suffers another crisis and decides to break away from film and theater, and devote herself to writing.

1960: A one-off return to theater for Pirandello's *Liolà*, directed by her friend Silverio Blasi.

1962 (spring): First suicide attempt. Goliarda is hospitalized in a psychiatric asylum, where she is given electric shock treatment. When she is discharged, a young analyst, Ignazio Majore, starts daily psychoanalysis therapy with her in her home.

1963: A three-month stay in Ravello. Goliarda embarks on a cycle of autobiographical writings (*Lettera aperta*, *Il filo di mezzogiorno* [Midday Thread], and *L'arte del dubbio*) which will continue until 1968 and allows her to explore significant events in her life.

1964: With his professional confidence in ruins, perhaps because of the relationship he started with

Goliarda and then abruptly broke off, Ignazio Majore abandons his career and his patients. Goliarda makes a second suicide attempt and spends several days in a coma.

1965: Goliarda separates from Citto Maselli. On Ignazio Majore's advice, she lives with a nurse by her side for two years.

1967–69: *Lettera aperta* and then *Il filo di mezzogiorno* are published by Garzanti. Goliarda throws herself fervently into writing *L'arte della gioia*.

1975–79: Goliarda meets Angelo Pellegrino, with whom she will collaborate until the end of her life. In 1978, the couple undertake a long journey on the Trans-Siberian railway, traveling across Russia and China.

1979: Goliarda and Angelo are married. The finished manuscript of *L'arte della gioia* is rejected by almost every Italian publishing company. Sandro Pertini, an old friend of her mother's and now president of the Italian republic, discreetly intervenes with the publisher Feltrinelli, to no avail.

1980: Goliarda has another breakdown. She is arrested following a jewelry theft in a friend's apartment and is held in Rebibbia's women's prison.

1983: *L'università di Rebibbia* is published by Rizzoli. It is a great success, but Rizzoli still refuse to publish *L'arte della gioia*.

1984: Goliarda finishes writing *Meeting in Positano* (*Appuntamento a Positano*). It will not be published in her lifetime.

1987: *Le certezze del dubbio* is published by Pellicanolibri.

1994: The first part of *L'arte della gioia* is published by Stampa Alternativa.

1996 (August 30): Goliarda Sapienza dies at her home in Gaeta after a fall in the house.

1998: Angelo Pellegrino reconstitutes the full text of *L'arte della gioia* and it is published posthumously. It goes unnoticed.

2002: Thanks again to Angelo Pellegrino's work, the collection *Destino coatto* is published by Empirìa.

2006: The rediscovery of Goliarda Sapienza in Italy reveals several significant unpublished texts. The prestigious publishing company Einaudi officially announces that it is committed to publishing the author's complete works.